CRUEL AS THE GRAVE

1-17-03

CRUEL AS THE GRAVE

Meg Elizabeth Atkins

Chivers Press • **Thorndike Press**
Bath, England **Waterville, Maine USA**

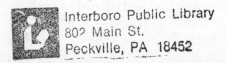

This Large Print edition is published by Chivers Press, England, and by Thorndike Press, USA.

Published in 2002 in the U.K. by arrangement with the author c/o Juliet Burton Literary Agency.

Published in 2002 in the U.S. by arrangement with Flambard Press.

U.K. Hardcover ISBN 0–7540–7440–4 (Chivers Large Print)
U.K. Softcover   ISBN 0–7540–7441–2 (Camden Large Print)
U.S. Softcover   ISBN 0–7862–4586–7 (Nightingale Series Edition)

The text of this Large Print edition is unabridged.
Other aspects of the book may vary from the original edition.

Set in 16 pt. New Times Roman.

Printed in Great Britain on acid-free paper.

British Library Cataloguing in Publication Data available

Library of Congress Cataloging-in-Publication Data

Atkins, Meg Elizabeth.
    Cruel as the grave / Meg Elizabeth Atkins.
      p. cm.
    ISBN 0–7862–4586–7 (lg. print : sc : alk. paper)
    1. Police—England—Cheshire—Fiction. 2. Cheshire
    (England)—Fiction. 3. Large type books. I. Title.
    PR6051.T5 C78 2002
    823'.914—dc21   2002075728

To Roger Forsdyke

in memory of Ms Grace Notes

R.I.P.

For love is strong as death; jealousy cruel as the grave.

Song of Solomon

CHAPTER ONE

Report in *The Chatfield Argus,* October 1990

A woman's body was discovered in the River Chat on Friday. The police have issued a description of the woman and are appealing for witnesses. They say that she had suffered various injuries but are not yet releasing full details, nor will they be specific about the cause of death. The body was discovered in the river early Friday morning, not far from a car park frequented by Hambling courting couples. Mrs Margaret Corning, a local resident, was walking her spaniels when she spotted the body, caught up amongst the branches of a tree on the river bank, face down in the reeds close to the edge of the river.

Speaking from her home in Chestnut Drive, Hambling, Mrs Corning said that at first she thought it was a brightly coloured plastic bag or sheet that had fallen in the river. She only realised it was a body when the water billowed the plastic to one side and she could see a pair of legs in white wellington boots.

At Chatfield police station, the officer in charge of the enquiry, Chief Inspector Sheldon Hunter, said that they had yet to establish whether foul play had been involved, but are treating the death as suspicious. The deceased

1

woman is described as being in her forties, about 5' 4" tall, well built, with bleached blonde hair. When recovered, she was wearing a red plastic raincoat, white plastic boots and see-through plastic rainhood. Anybody who has been in the area of the car park or towpath near Miller's Bridge in the last few days are asked to contact the police on 0113 621111. They would be pleased to speak to anyone who has information which may assist them with their enquiries. All communications, they stress, will be treated in the strictest confidence.

*   *   *

In his office at Chatfield sub-divisional headquarters, Chief Inspector Sheldon Hunter studied the photograph and description of the unknown woman.

There was something obscurely troubling about her face—the fuzzy image airbrushed by the sorcerer's apprentice. On the surface of his mind a comparison formed: Litter Lil, said to hang around street corners for the purpose of servicing the dustbin men. Had she really? Or was that just one of your friendly neighbourhood slanders? It would never have occurred to him to question it all those years ago—as a lad on a tough council estate he was concerned with survival, not the abstract reconciliation of truth and reputation.

The fleeting likeness disposed of, he turned

2

to conjecture.

Final cause of death: drowning. Multiple injuries to legs, back and head. Leg injuries before death, others post-mortem—to be expected with her being buffeted about by the water . . . That made him pause. Something that didn't quite add up. Wouldn't it have made more sense the other way around? He made a note to speak to the pathologist.

Fabric gloves—ripped. Damage to hands—could have been caused as she fell into the water, trying to save herself . . . Or could they conceivably be defence wounds? Vaginal swab showed she had not recently had intercourse.

Miller's Bridge. Hambling. A mellow, prosperous market town. Geographical distance from Chatfield, twenty-eight miles. Social distance, immeasurable.

What was a red plastic raincoat doing in Laura Ashley country?

Because she must have gone in the river round about there. Two miles upriver, to the north, the weir would have caught her. South below the weir, the river Chat ran fast and straight to just beyond Miller's Bridge. There the banks curved, jutted, rose and fell, forming the willow-trailed inlets, the glades, the whispering leafy walks that made the place such a beauty spot.

It was around this area the search for evidence had been concentrated, yielding nothing. Hunter could not justify throwing any

3

more money and manpower into a situation that could turn out to have a straightforward, innocent explanation. He tried, and failed to imagine anything straightforward about a lone woman on an autumn night of teeming rain wandering about a beauty spot minus her handbag.

It had to be there, that handbag. To his way of thinking no woman ever went out without one. Not 'out' in the sense that undoubtedly applied here—carefully dressed in her cheap, bright clothes, her pathetic jewellery; her face made up, her nails varnished. She had hardworking hands. Her body was slack and spreading—a stranger to aerobic classes. Her brassily dyed hair flaunted its message: *look at me. I'm still young. I'm still game.*

Not any more, you poor cow.

In the urban miscellany of Chatfield she would merely be one of a crowd, but in Hambling—in that part of Hambling—she would be as strident as a fairground on a Saturday night. But no one had seen her. Yet. Hunter looked hopefully at the poster intended to identify her, then absently at Detective Sergeant James Collier, who had just come in.

Hunter said, 'There are houses on either side of the bridge. Plenty of passing traffic during the day. Green wellies and waxed jacket no one would notice her. But red and white plastic, for God's sake. So it had to be after dark.'

Newly promoted—a sideways move from uniformed sergeant—Collier's working relationship with Hunter was brief, but already he had been at the receiving end of a mind in continual conversation with itself. Coming in on cue could be tricky; not on this occasion, fortunately, with the poster prominent on Hunter's desk. 'She could have been taken there by car, dropped off close to the spot. Or walked across the fields. There are footpaths . . .'

'She'd have been ankle deep in mud, this weather. I know, there's no way of telling. She wasn't in the river long but any marks or deposits there might have been on those shiny plastic surfaces had been scoured off by silt and river water. If only we knew who she was we could get started. You haven't come in here to tell me she's turned up on the wanted-missing persons index?'

'Not so far, still looking. I wondered about the likelihood of this turning into murder, guv. Just in case we have to get Holmes up and running.'

'Holmes,' Hunter sighed. Home Office Large Major Enquiry System. 'I'm beginning to suspect you have an unnatural attachment to the damn thing. I'd never have let you go on that refresher course if I'd known you'd come back besotted.'

Aware that his DCI regarded computers

with mystified respect, Collier settled for looking innocent and saying nothing.

'Oh, well . . .' Hunter growled. He stood up—a big man, a physical presence that could be intimidating or reassuring, whatever the occasion demanded; but always powerful. 'Come on, time we had a cup of coffee and a talk about starting to make a few contingency plans. At the moment, I'm regarding it as a suspicious death; it wouldn't take much to step it up into a full murder enquiry.'

Half a dozen paces down the corridor Hunter halted at the sound of his telephone, audible despite multiple layers of crime files and other debris. He went swiftly back, burrowed for the receiver, ignoring the gravity-induced cascade of papers. 'Detective Chief Inspector Hunter.'

'That body in the river—' The voice was androgynous: a light tenor or husky contralto.

'May I ask who's speaking?'

'It's murder. And he lives in Hambling.'

Disguised voice. Crank. But Hunter was suddenly alert. 'Who does?'

CHAPTER TWO

A house like a secret. Helen Willoughby's gift to her goddaughter, Liz Farrell. Helen was doubtful—such an *odd* little place, but Liz,

6

enchanted, said *please*, Helen.

It stood on the edge of Hambling, on a tree-shaded, small road called Bellfield, where the houses had long established gardens retreating behind shrubberies. Liz's house was the last one, on a corner where the road went out to pasture, woods, the sheltering rise of hills. Every Monday morning during term time she locked up and drove the two hundred miles to teach history at Wilton House Girls' College in Surrey, returning on Friday evening. At first she worried about leaving the house to itself—not about burglaries or squatters, she had never in her thirty-four years personally known anyone to whom such things happened or, if she had, she preferred not to remember. It was a possessive worry, made up of the pride of ownership and the vulnerable sense of being out of her shell.

On the drenched October evening when she had, unusually, been away for a fortnight, it was apparent to her on her return that he had been there again.

Reggie had been entertaining one of his women in her house.

Why couldn't he take them to a hotel? Somewhere? Anywhere . . .

Because there had been some silliness once, just after she'd moved in.—'Reggie, I chose this house because I can get away with anything. Orgies. Anything. Don't tell Helen. She'd be devastated to think she'd financed a

7

knocking shop.' Liz loved teasing Reggie—the attractive, open face shocked and delighted. 'I say, Liz . . . the neighbours, dash it.' 'Reggie, the geography is on my side—' he was not very bright and always had to have the obvious explained—'you drive along Bellfield, most of the houses are set so far back no one can see you, even if they can hear you. You turn the corner here—slip into the drive. But who's to know? You could have just driven straight on.' Reggie, painfully thinking it over (well into his forties he managed, always, to stay Helen's little brother), said, 'You'll be telling me next you're going to rent it out for immoral purposes.' 'Who said anything about rent? Free to pals . . .'

Being Reggie, he took her at her word. He knew where the spare key was hidden, knew when she would be away. When she found out she was exasperated but forgiving. His apology conveyed the hurt of the unjustly accused.— 'But you said no one would know.' 'Dammit, Reggie *I* know. It's *my* house.' 'It's all right about the neighbours, then? I wouldn't—I mean—your reputation and all that.' She wanted to shout *bugger the neighbours*, but with his muddled gallantry he had got hold of the idea that the issue at stake was her good name and was anxious to reassure her it would be his first consideration. She tried to extract a promise he wouldn't do it again, but Reggie's promises were all of a piece with his inefficient escapades, his boyish charm. And she had the mad feeling he might make some half-strangulated statement about a Chap Having Needs and she would become hysterical.

In a context of furtive sexuality it was unthinkable Helen's name should be mentioned. Reggie and Helen were embalmed in a lost era. They had survived a dictatorial father whose notions of conduct forced them into a straitjacket of behaviour they were incapable of challenging. Freed by the old man's death, Helen ran the house, mothered Reggie, entertained friends, pursued her interests. She encouraged Reggie in what she called his 'attachments'—fleeting social affairs that seemed to Liz devoid of physicality. For a woman whose life had been so restricted, Helen was remarkably broad-minded, referring to Liz and her contemporaries rather wistfully as 'splendid young people'. But she was mistress of a gracious home; immutable standards governed her every personal circumstance. Reggie, sensitive to her feelings, would never introduce her to anyone she might consider unsuitable—worse still, common.

'Well, Ms Whoever-you-are,' Liz said aloud in the silence of her trespassed house. 'It's a fair bet you're not one of Helen's splendid young people.' Could Reggie's secret tastes be disgraceful? Sixteen-year-old girls? Raucous old tarts? Perhaps the *she* was a *he*? Who cared about that, it wasn't illegal.

9

Mystified, tracking the course of his intrusion, Liz could never avoid the evidence that neither of the two beds had ever been used. Did they do it downstairs? Standing up? Did they just talk?

Whatever . . . she was thoroughly fed up with having her domestic arrangements open to the gaze of a stranger. To cheer herself up she went into the third bedroom. This was her workroom, the clutter was inspirational: sewing machine, dressmaker's dummy, bolts of cloth, garments half made on hangers, draped over chairs. Her joy was the wardrobe work she did for Hambling Amateur Dramatic Society, and in the toybox absurdity of this room, amongst masks, jewelled scabbards, glittering slippers, fans, wigs, she lost herself for hours.

Content for the moment merely to look, touch, pick things up and put them down again, she went into her bedroom and became absorbed in the routine of unpacking.

She had a face full of feeling, sometimes treacherously giving too much away: delicate and narrow, long-lidded eyes and beautifully shaped mouth. Her skin had a pale golden tone; her short, softly waved hair a deeper gold. She was too tall and too thin, childhood an embarrassment of barging about and knocking things over—demonstrating her mother's assertion she would always be clumsy. Helen, wasting no words on sympathy, paid for dancing lessons. In time, Liz's flying limbs acquired co-ordination and the distinction of an impulsive grace. Her tendencies were slapdash—jobs half finished, objects in unlikely places—even so, this was *her* house, her comfort was in its familiar ordering.

Until she sat down at her dressing table, reached forward to adjust the mirror and then sat immobile.

The triple mirror was arranged to suit her. It was never moved because no one sat there, except her. Now the centre panel was tilted down, the side panels adapted to someone much shorter, who sat in a different way.

The creeping unease was disproportionate, chilling, filling the room.

As if the unknown woman sat there with her.

Aloud, she said, 'Damn you, Reggie.'

*   *   *

The relentless rain was enough to subdue anyone's spirits.

In the sitting room, after supper, she switched on the floodlights that illuminated the garden and stood with a glass of wine looking out through the french window. Autumn was depositing its litter in heaps of leaves, tangles of dead branches. Everything was drenched, swamped, drowning.

The phone rang. It was Paula, Helen's younger sister.

'Liz, isn't it frightful?' Paula had no truck with the niceties of hallo-how-are-you? She used the phone as a form of sandbagging. 'It could be a case of police harassment. It needs looking into.'

Liz stifled a sigh. Paula lived in the centre of Hambling; she had been divorced, gladiatorially, some years previously; her two storming daughters were packed off to boarding school (not hers, Liz always thanked God). Paula did voluntary work, strenuously, grappling with the Council, or the DHSS, or someone likely to give her a good fight.

'Look, Paula, it's late and I'm pretty tired. Would you like to tell me in the morning?'

The sharp intake of breath, suggesting outrage; then, after a short silence, reasonably, 'Well, of course, you don't know. We didn't want to phone you at school and worry you.'

'About what? It's not Helen, is it? There's nothing wrong?'

'Depends on what you call wrong. Personally, I don't see what could be right in a situation like this.'

'What situation?' Liz's grip on the receiver tightened. There was nothing Paula enjoyed so much as being the bearer of bad news; it would all be about nothing. 'Is Helen all right?'

'Oh, Helen . . . well, you know Helen. Granite gentility. Deal with anything. I should think you'd be more concerned about Reggie.'

'Reggie? Paula, what *is* it?'

'That woman whose body was found in the Chat, at Miller's Bridge. I know it only rated a line or two in the nationals but, after all, it's on your doorstep.'

'Miller's Bridge? Hardly. Well, it's . . . No, I don't know anything about a body. What on earth has this to do with Reggie?'

'Well, *I'll* take a great deal of convincing he has *anything* to do with it. The police think differently. When they took him in for questioning—

Liz sat down suddenly.

'—you know how non-assertive he is. I'm sure he wasn't properly informed of his rights. I can tell you, if I'd been there—'

'Paula, what are you saying? Reggie's been *arrested*? I don't believe it—Oh, God, I must go, Helen, she'll be—'

'I don't want you to bother her at this time of night, she has a bad enough job sleeping as it is.'

'Oh, you mean—you're there with her.'

'With her? No. Why should I be? I'm at home.'

'But, she's all alone—'

'No, she's not, Reggie's there.'

I'm going insane. 'Paula, you said Reggie had been arrested.'

'No, I didn't. I said he'd been taken in for questioning. They let him out again—well,

13

they had to.'

Liz yelled, 'Why didn't you tell me that before?'

'Liz, if you become hysterical, I'll hang up. This is typical of you, flying off the handle at the least provocation. I don't know what good you think you'll be to Helen in this state. You'll only upset her.'

'Me. Upset Helen,' Liz snarled.

'She needs kid-glove treatment at the moment. She's coping marvellously really. And after all, it's nothing cataclysmic. When there's a murder the police question everyone, it's a matter of routine.'

Liz said stubbornly, 'They don't question *everyone*, they have to have a reason, surely. Look, when did all this happen?'

'Um—Thursday night—her body wasn't found till the Friday morning. The town was agog. I mean, a murder in Hambling. My dear, how common. You should have been here. You were away last weekend, weren't you? Where did you go?'

'Dorset,' Liz said at random. Where she had been and why was none of Paula's business. 'But, about Reggie—'

'Yes, well. The police wanted to know his movements on the Thursday night—the day before her body was found. He didn't *have* to go to the police station to make a statement, that "voluntary" business is all crap. I mean, your average, law-abiding citizen is far from clear about his rights—not to mention someone as generally hopeless as Reggie. Anyway, I want you to go round in the morning, it's essential you let Helen know where you stand.'

'Where I what?'

'There's a tremendous amount of talk—insinuations. I can dismiss it, but Helen and Reggie are so concerned for the good name of—'

'Insinuations?'

'Don't be dense. You know the sort of thing . . . no smoke without a fire. Ridiculous, I know. But it's how people react, human nature being what it is, pretty ghastly on the whole. I've been as positive and supportive as I can but it's about time Helen and Reggie had a little input from you. It's just unfortunate you chose to be away when you'd have been more use at home.'

'I could scarcely anticipate something like this.'

'My point exactly. So you'll go round to Woodside first thing, won't you? They need one of us and I shall be away for a couple of days.'

'Of course I will,' Liz said, responding to the genuine note of concern in Paula's voice.

'Good. I *have* to be in Eastbourne. I should have gone this afternoon but I hung on till you got back. As it is I'll leave at the crack of dawn tomorrow. It's Bess and Alfred's golden wedding, they're having a full gathering of the clans . . .'

And it was unthinkable Paula should not be there. Bess and Alfred Warner—distant relatives of the Willoughbys—had taken care of Paula after her mother's early death— a temporary arrangement that became permanent. At that time they lived near Hambling and had young children of their own.

Their tribalism engulfed Paula, providing her with what she once described to Liz as 'the rough and tumble of family life, the loving and sharing, the lessons of give and take. Something you never had, Liz, and Helen doesn't even know about.' The Warners made much of rituals: weddings, christenings, anniversaries. As the junior Warners proliferated there were many such occasions and Paula was conscientious about attending them, even after her foster-parents moved to Eastbourne.

'. . . I was supposed to help with the arrangements, it's a lot for Bess and Alfred, but it means so much to them to have everyone there. Michael's coming over from Brussels with his new wife and his two and her two, and Gloria's over from Canada with Bob and the twins . . .'

Shoals of names surged past Liz, meaning little or nothing. She made the occasional automatic response, all that was necessary

16

when Paula was in full throat. But at last, the catalogue of unknowable people marrying, divorcing, breeding, travelling had its usual mind-stunning effect and when it was finally concluded she could put down the receiver and go to bed in a calmer frame of mind. Before she did so, she looked in the two copies of the free papers that had been delivered during her absence and in the recent one read the report of the discovery of the woman's body. No name was given and the description meant nothing to her.

Her descent into sleep was tangled with thoughts of Reggie, what to do about him and his . . . what? Assignations? Then she came upon a solution. She would hide the key in another place, where he wouldn't find it. Of course—warn him what she had done, to spare him any last minute embarrassment.

She woke with a start, in darkness, with the desperate feeling: *something's happened, something's happened . . .*

Then she realised it was merely that the rain had stopped at last.

CHAPTER THREE

The Willoughby house, built in the Edwardian age to accommodate a large family and necessary servants, stood on Woodside—a winding road of spinneys and grass clearings. When Mrs Willoughby died shortly after Paula's birth, Helen took on the duties of housekeeper, hostess for her father, nurse to her father's invalid parents, mother to Reggie. The infant Paula's noisy and unremitting demands for attention proved too much for everyone—it was then she was sent to the Warners. Mr Willoughby had an aversion to children; Helen and Reggie had been kept out of his way until they were rational enough to meet his standards of correct behaviour. He cultivated the image of a refined, successful man; domestic life was shaped to his requirements, which were of unyielding selfishness. He never laid a hand on his children in anger or affection; his cruelties were verbal, his disdain annihilating.

Reared in the tradition of obedience, Helen never made the least gesture of subversion. When the long-lived Willoughby grandparents eventually obliged everyone by dying within a few months of one another she was free—as her father saw it—to devote herself to his ever more fastidious needs. If she wept for the years running away with her youth and her life, the essence of her individual self, she did so in private. Paula, visiting, urged rebellion. Growing up in the freedom of education and opportunity, she despised Helen's effacement. 'You're turning into a dried up old maid. You want to *fulfil* yourself. Get away.' But where?

Helen was a superb house-keeper but her accomplishments did not equip her to provide for herself.

After retirement, Mr Willoughby suffered a stroke, declined physically and mentally, the peevishness of age uncovering seams of malice in his unpleasant nature. 'He's a vicious bastard. How can you stand it? You know he's going ga-ga. Put him in a nursing home,' Paula said to Helen. 'I couldn't, he'd make a frightful fuss. Paula, it's sweet of you to try to help but, truly, I think it best if you didn't see him again. It makes him so—confused, and difficult to handle.' 'Confused? What in God's name is he drivelling about? I just pretend to listen, I've more than enough trouble of my own at the moment.' Paula was distracted by the break-up of her marriage and the exercise of using her daughters as weapons. She suggested Reggie make himself useful—'Father's only got to set eyes on him to have a seizure. With any luck it might be fatal.'

But Helen bore the burden alone, to the limit of her endurance. When the time came and she stood at her father's graveside her neat little body was skin and bone, her face haunted. Liz's mother—Helen's cousin—was at the funeral. She said, 'Imagine her taking it so badly. Anyone would think she cared for the old brute.' Liz snapped back that Helen was worn out—'None of us helped her enough.' 'Well, she can help herself now. You know she's got the lot.' Liz's mother, an unhappy woman with a distraught personal life, could never forgive Helen for stealing Liz's affection; it never occurred to her that if she'd had any to give, her daughter wouldn't have sought it elsewhere. 'Anyway, you stupid girl, how could you have *helped*? Eh? He couldn't stand the sight of you, you'd only have made things worse. Not that that ever stops you. Do you know what Helen says about you?' With spiteful mimicry, Liz's mother spoke in Helen's caressing tones—'Dear Liz *always* does the wrong thing for the right reasons.'

*   *   *

And that morning, holding Helen in a firm hug, Liz said, 'I could have rushed here last night but it was so late when Paula phoned. That *would* have been the wrong thing for the right reasons, wouldn't it?'

Helen emerged from Liz's embrace: slim, with a small-boned, intelligent face; eyes that were still beautiful; her make-up was careful, her hair dyed a becoming, almost natural brown. Her composure, reassuringly intact, indicated that whatever happened, she would deal with it. 'I was up with Reggie in his room, so glad to see it was your car in the drive. My sensible Liz. You appreciate I refuse to make much of this.'

20

'Of course . . .' Talking together, they crossed the shining parquet of the wide hall with its beautiful Chinese rugs. The wide staircase went up on shallow treads to turn on a graceful half landing. Helen had made no concessions to modernity here: the centre-placed floral carpet snapped down at each tread by brass stair-rods, gleaming, fleur-de-lis shaped; on either side the expanses of mahogany, every grain, every polished surface announcing its quality. On the half landing, beneath a wide sash window, velvet curtained—a carved oak blanket chest; a gilded rococo pot spilling an exuberant fern; an enormous dinner gong . . . *Aunt Helen, it's lunch time, please may I bang the gong, please . . .*

They went into the kitchen, where Helen made coffee. She said, 'It's so hard on Reggie. So unfair. And he's been awfully brave.'

Liz took this to mean he had squared his jaw and gone out to face the world. Why should he not? He worked at something dull in a large complex of Government buildings known as Little Whitehall. His father had insisted he go into the Civil Service—it being the ideal institution to absorb Reggie's inefficiency and limit his capacity for getting into messes. She asked if they were giving him plenty of support at work—she could hardly say they must be overjoyed to have something interesting to talk about at last, and thanked

21

heaven she'd saved herself from such crassness when Helen murmured, 'Poor lamb. He's not cut out to be the object of sensational curiosity. There's a great deal of unpleasantness about something like this. People make jokes. They whisper. He *really did try*, but it was too awful. Now he won't even leave the house. He feels he can't walk around town without being pointed out.'

'Helen—this is awful.'

'It is *essential* that we keep things in proportion. All this will blow over, we must just stay calm.'

'Calm—yes. But, Helen, I do find it confusing. I mean, that woman's body at Miller's Bridge—what *on earth* has it got to do with Reggie?'

'Nothing, of course, it was all a misunderstanding. Bring the tray, darling,' Helen said briskly.

Obediently, Liz carried the tray into the garden room. Helen's father, enraged by the prospect of death extinguishing his dictatorship, made Helen promise never to change anything in the house. She promised. After his death, a decent interlude, she began work.

The house had beautiful proportions but it was gloomy, inconveniently old-fashioned, stifled by the air of sickness, old age, outworn memories. Helen let in the light, filled it with comfort and colour. The garden room, her favourite, was entirely her creation. Long, low-ceilinged, panelled in white wood; one wall entirely floor to ceiling windows; she had chosen the most delicate furniture, sweet-pea colours of tender clarity, so that even in winter the room breathed the air of lost summers, of summers to come. The view of the garden was a gauze of autumn sunlight, shimmering away to a curtain of willows.

The two women sat close together. In a house so spacious and solidly built, conversations could not be overheard, yet they spoke softly—Helen would allow nothing to disrupt the serenity she had created. She said, 'Now, before we go into this tiresome business. Tell me about last weekend. Did you . . .' A pause of perfect discretion. 'Did you call it all off?'

'Yes. We walked miles in a kind of ferocious silence, then went back to the hotel, and he'd make this dreadful fuss . . .' Liz talked, feeling now nothing but relief, glad to unburden herself about the difficulty of getting rid of a lover who didn't want to go. Helen listened, murmured. Her sympathy was enveloping, her understanding remarkable in that she had never—as far as Liz knew—had anything beyond mere friendship with a man in her life. Her father would never have permitted anything of the kind; but after his death . . .

Liz guarded hopes. Helen was still beautiful—and last summer had brought

Wilfred—with all the sexiness and wit and looks of a man half his seventy years. But the summer ended, and he went back to Hampshire . . . Liz spared a regretful thought for Wilfred before saying firmly, 'Enough about me. It's over. I'm available again. Come along. Tell.'

'Where shall I begin? The police enquiries. Unfortunately, I wasn't in when they called, or I'm sure it wouldn't have happened. You see, Reggie kept getting mixed up about where he'd been that particular Thursday night. He went over to Robert's at Midham but Robert wasn't in so he'd driven around. Then he said—no, that was another evening. Then he said he'd been *here* all the time.'

'What a mess. Were you at home?'

'No, it was my turn to keep old Martha Riggs company. Reggie and I went out more or less together—immediately after dinner— and he didn't come home till quite late. I heard him, I can't be sure what the time was— past midnight. Liz, we're used to him, we know he's easily confused, and he gets intimidated and rather silly if he thinks he's being accused of something.'

'Yes. But anyone who doesn't know him would think the worst.'

'Quite. He had absolutely nothing to do with that unfortunate person. No one even knows who she is, or what she was doing round here—she certainly wasn't local. But he got into such a tangle the officer asked him to go along to the police station and make a statement.'

'Asked him? Paula gave me the impression he'd been frogmarched.'

'Well, Paula. She *has* tried to help.'

'Oh, God . . .'

'Yes.'

The short silence brimmed with perfect understanding as together they contemplated the seething nature of Paula's helpfulness.

Liz said optimistically, 'She'll lose interest when the drama goes out of it. But I still don't understand. Why pick on Reggie in the first place?'

'Apparently they had some reason to believe he was near Miller's Bridge that night, at the time it happened. I suppose really they wanted to know if he'd seen anyone about or seen . . . her.'

For the first time, Helen wavered. The reality of the dead woman, a drowned woman, unknown, unclaimed, invaded the lovely room. Liz, driving over Miller's Bridge scarcely half an hour before, had felt curiosity, nothing more. Now it was as if this woman had suddenly acquired a personal significance, was capable of wrenching their lives out of shape.

A *frisson*. Liz would have dismissed it, had not Helen continued to sit, tense, gazing out at the garden. Liz thought, she's hiding so much distress. Helen moved, self-possession

25

regained, spoke with genteel emphasis. 'It was nonsense. He was nowhere near there. He *did* go to Robert's, and that's miles away, as you know. And because Robert wasn't in he went for a drink at the Feathers, then that pretty place by the village pond at Crale. He wasn't exactly *with* anyone but he was seen by people who recognised him.'

As Liz asked questions and Helen explained in more detail, a picture emerged of Reggie spending an aimless evening, drinking alone. He would not have been over the limit, he was conscientious about drinking and driving, but he was a social creature, hating his own company. All his adult life he had applied himself to leisure with the tenacity of the empty-headed; he had any number of places to go to be with friends.

'I take it Robert wasn't expecting him?'

'No. If he had been, this disagreeable business would have been avoided. If I hadn't gone out to sit with poor old Martha Riggs, Reggie could have come home—but he knew the house would be empty, and he does so hate being alone. If . . .'

Liz was about to say, dreadfully, that it was all water under the bridge, when Helen forestalled her by saying firmly, 'However, we can't turn back the clock, we must be sensible and let everything return to normal.'

Liz was wondering if Reggie really had just taken it into his head to drive out to Robert's or if he might have been expecting to meet someone at her cottage and there'd been a mix-up. His life was ambushed by mix-ups—present him with the unexpected and he dithered. There was nothing she dare say to Helen about it—after all, Helen had been deceived by them both and the only relief for guilt Liz could find was the silliness of the whole business. In the midst of her worry about Reggie, this trivial business was the last thing Helen needed to know.

But, Liz considered, Reggie could be in need of a little reassurance—if his conscience was troubling him, or he was afraid she might let something slip. Just a word, not to make an issue of it—*never fear, old chap, your secret is safe with me.* She put her hand on Helen's, an encouraging pat. 'I'll go up and have a chat with him, shall I?'

'No.' Helen's thin fingers curved, clutching. 'No, he doesn't want to talk to anyone.'

Liz was so shocked she could only say, stupidly, 'But—it's me—'

'Oh, darling, how could I be so tactless? Don't be hurt. Let me explain. It was frightful for him—taken away in a police car, held in an interview room, which he said was ghastly. Questioned—nothing like it has ever happened to him in his life. It's knocked the stuffing out of him completely.'

Cruel to point out there was hardly any stuffing to begin with. Instead, Liz said gently,

'But this is serious. He can't shut himself away, he'll make himself ill. Has he seen the doctor?'

'Oh, yes, I made sure of that. Tranquillisers, advice to take things easy. But, we've had a good talk. What I think is important at the moment is for him to do what he wants to do. He needs a breathing space. So we've arranged he'll go to Cheltenham and stay with Uncle William.'

'The old sea-dog . . .' A retired naval chaplain, surreally absentminded, Uncle William was adored by everyone. 'Well, yes, he should be able to put Reggie together again. But, Helen, are you sure it's a good thing?' Reggie was running away. They would not say it but they both knew it.

'No, darling, but at the moment it's the only thing. I shall drive him this afternoon and stay over and come back tomorrow or Monday. You do understand, don't you? Just a short time away will do him so much good. A week, perhaps, while all this blows over. He needs to—steady himself.'

No. He needed to go off like a child, to somewhere where no one knew he had been naughty; to someone kind, who would spoil him. And then to come back when Helen had smoothed everything out, put their life back into shape. As if nothing had happened.

CHAPTER FOUR

She was a maternal body; enjoyed a good gossip, cuffed her children and grandchildren into shape. She'd been known to manhandle local louts who got in her way—but she had to steel herself to enter the gleaming vestibule of Chatfield police station. This modern stuff was all very well; the old nick had been homelier—although she'd had as little as possible to do with that.

From a heroically veteran handbag she drew the latest copy of the free weekly newspaper and said to the desk sergeant, 'I know who she is. This woman. Beattie Booth. None of it's nothing to do with me, but if someone doesn't speak up, he'll get away with it and he oughtn't to be allowed.'

*   *   *

'Now then, Mrs Wellbed,' Hunter said.

Defensive, determined, she took her time, glanced about his office, establishing her importance at being there. Her eyes came to rest on Hunter, sharpening. 'I know you, don't I? Enid Hunter's lad.'

'That's right.'

'I remember when you moved off the estate. Your mam came into a bit of money from—

her brother, weren't it? *And* his house. So you moved. Went up in the world.'

Modestly enough: a characterless semi in a suburb of numbing respectability . . . He resented the lost lawlessness of the streets, returned whenever he could. But time and new horizons sorted that out.

'You always was an untidy bugger,' Mrs Wellbed said, gazing at his chaotic desk.

He grinned, 'I can't argue with you there. So, she was a friend—Beattie Booth.'

'Friend, no. I scarce said two words to her in years. Seen her about often enough. And I hear tell of her through our Marge and her lot, they're all regulars at the Prince Albert. And what *they* thought when she didn't turn up Friday night after all her big talk was that he'd just ditched her. Well, a feller like that—well-off, posh—answer to a maiden's prayer. Not that she was no maiden since she was fourteen. She hadn't let herself go, mind, and when she was dolled up she was worth a second look, I'll say that. When she was a girl she was a looker—like her mother'd been—but you know what happened to her.'

Hunter, listening carefully, made a show of amused helplessness. 'Hang on, Mrs Wellbed, I'm not taking all this in.'

'It's what you're for, isn't it?'

'I sometimes wonder. Now, if you'll just bear with me—' He would have tried charm, but it wouldn't work on Mrs Wellbed. She needed to look down on him, get her own back for his desertion, all those years ago, of her and her kind. His own kind. The decision, then, had not been his. She knew that, of course, but refused to take it into account. 'Can I just start with a few details. Beattie Booth. Miss? Mrs?'

'Miss. But not for want of trying.'

'And her address?'

'How would I know? Used to be Owen Street, when she was a kid—well, you remember all round there.'

—Of course he remembered. Terraces, yards, alleys, survivals of the Industrial Revolution, and his own roaring, depersonalised council estate—the whole area designated Greenacres, in harsh mockery of forgotten fields.

' . . . then, when it were pulled down, her and her mam were rehoused in the Causeway. You know.'

He knew. And like everyone marvelled how a new development could be an immediate slum. There was one thing to be said for Causeway—you could get away from it bloody quick. On the thundering arterial roads that hemmed it in. Not for nothing was it known as Suicide Row.

Hunter thought about Causeway, briefly consulted his mental gazetteer of Chatfield. 'The Prince Albert's not her local, then?'

'*Course* not. But it *were.* Not everyone as moves away goes for good. Some folk like to keep in touch. A few as was shifted to Causeway still comes round.'

'And she was a regular at the Prince Albert?'

'Every Friday.'

'With this man?'

'*With* him.' She made a sharp, scornful sound, like a swallowed laugh. 'With him. That'd be the day. No one ever set eyes on him.'

'Did she mention his name?'

'Not her. Played it close to her chest.'

A constable brought tea in, properly, on a tray, with matching cups and milkjug and sugar bowl. A small attention, visibly bringing out the best in Mrs Wellbed. Stirring in three fortifying teaspoons of sugar, she said reflectively, 'Y'know, I said to our Marge once—does he bloody exist? Cos they used to call him Mr Moonshine. And our Marge said, "I've wondered, mam, specially at first when she just dropped hints. Wouldn't put it past the silly cow to make the whole thing up. Then I weren't so sure. There's *summat*, mam. Definite." Cos Beattie were—different. She'd got money to spend, bought herself some new clothes, new handbag, *and* not from one of them Oxfam places.'

. . . the problematic handbag. Where was it? . . .

'Did she have a car?'

'*Car*!' This time Mrs Wellbed's laughter erupted, shrill as a train whistle. 'She was on

Social Security. Lost her job a while back at Norton's Packaging—they laid fifty off. Time I knew her, when she lived in Owen Street, she did cleaning jobs. Car? When did she ever have money for a car? When did I? Buses do us.'

Buses. One of the roads by Causeway fed directly into the north-eastern section of the by-pass. Once on that . . . a straight journey to Hambling. Hambling bus station lay to the west of the town, close to the centre. Then, whether you went by car, taxi or pogo stick, Miller's Bridge lay a good two miles south-east. A long walk on a rainy night.

'You don't recollect her?' Mrs Wellbed asked. 'You'd be of an age, all you lads and lassies together. Owen Street wasn't far from you . . .'

'I've been trying to think.' He shook his head. 'I can't honestly say even her name means anything to me. What are we talking about—the fifties? The place was teeming with kids . . .' Territorial animals. It was risky wandering into the wrong street; asking for trouble if you set out on gang trespass. True, there were common meeting grounds where non-aggression pacts mysteriously operated— and in all that swarm of faces and names and comings and goings, he might have known the girl. Even so, it was unlikely she would be rediscoverable in the face of the woman—his fleeting recognition had been of a type, not an

33

individual. 'Has she any family round here still?'

'No. Last one were her cousin Muriel, took off with some feller, Newcastle or thereabouts. They wasn't speaking then on account of Muriel never giving much of a hand to help with Beattie's mam. Drove Beattie mad, the old woman did, specially later on—but Beattie soldiered on. Well, she'd no choice. But she didn't give in. That's what I mean . . .' Mrs Wellbed paused, perplexed; the point at which she wished to arrive evidently eluding her. 'She were working at Norton's when her mam died, so she had a chance after all them years, earn a bit of money, enjoy herself a bit. Then she was laid off—but before you know it, up she pops with this feller as was going to put her in clover . . . *That's* what I mean. She might have been a fool and a bit of a cow, and I can't say I had all that much time for her—but she deserved better than that. Drowned in some place with strangers all around her. All on account of a feller she was daft enough to listen to. She was like her mam where fellers was concerned. Unlucky. Dead unlucky.'

Beattie's antecedents were not Hunter's concern; however, with a decision forming in his mind, he allowed Mrs Wellbed to talk. She was too dedicated a gossip to need encouragement, or to notice how skilfully he directed her. When he was satisfied, he said, 'You've performed a valuable service in

34

coming in to see us, Mrs Wellbed, and I'm grateful. There's something you can do that will assist us even more. It's a favour, you're under no obligation and I'll quite understand if you refuse. Would you identify Beattie?'

She stared at him. He had probably established a record: the only man to render Mrs Wellbed speechless.

'You see, there's no immediate family available, as you said. You've known Beattie all her life; you're a sensible, reliable person. We can see to it straight away—I'll get a woman detective sergeant to go with you to the mortuary, and then afterwards you make a statement of identification. That is, if you'd be good enough, if it wouldn't distress you too much.'

She found her voice, subdued but determined. 'Nay, lad, it'll not be the first dead face I've looked on. Yes, yes, I'll do it.'

Of course she would—she had her reputation in the neighbourhood to consider. At the prospect of giddying fame, Mrs Wellbed squared her shoulders, grasped her handbag and, under Hunter's ironic eye, surged forth to do her civic duty.

*　　*　　*

'Right, we've got a name,' Hunter said to Collier. 'No, don't rush off and start playing with your appliance, I'm not sure yet where

35

we're going with this one, not till I've spoken to the pathologist. Beattie Booth. Miss. She lived at Causeway but we don't know where exactly. Get someone on to the DHSS, they'll let us have her address. As I understand it, she lived alone, a neighbour might have a key.'

'At Causeway?' Collier said expressively. No one handed round door keys in a combat zone.

'Mmm. Doubtful, but you can try. And I want a word with George Withers; find out from the control room when he's next on duty, will you?'

'He's the local beat bobby round the old Owen Street area, isn't he?

'Prince Albert. Our Marge, too.'

'Yes, guv.' Collier cast about with perfectly controlled incomprehension.

'On his patch.'

Unable to find a connection between such widely separated areas as Causeway and Owen Street, Collier struck out on his own. 'Hambling have been on, they've got someone who saw the woman on Thursday evening near Miller's Bridge. Taylor's checking up on it.'

'Good. Chase them up. And when you come back, I'll tell you about Mrs Wellbed.'

'Was she the—er—large lady with the handbag?'

Hunter narrowed his eyes. 'Watch out for that handbag, lad. It's brought down stronger men than you.'

'What I'm saying,' Hunter bellowed into the phone, 'those injuries to the legs . . . If there'd been a struggle before she went into the water . . . There were no indications in the immediate vicinity but the ground was so churned up it was difficult to tell.' He wondered if his voice or his patience would give way before the old boy turned up his hearing aid.

Matthew Ames, the pathologist, was nearing retirement and allegedly sensitive about his deafness. Knowing his demonic humour, Hunter suspected there were days when he set out deliberately to exhaust people or drive them mad with lengthy answers to questions they had not asked. Hunter experimented: a quiet, conversational tone. 'Are you having me on, you wicked old fart?'

The low whistle of a much-fiddled-with hearing aid preceded Ames's voice. 'I know the area. Charming. Beautiful old bridge, that low stone parapet. You've taken a look at it?'

'Not personally. What I want—'

'She was wearing calf-length boots; her raincoat came midway between calf and knee. Her tights were torn. The injuries extended up to the thighs and were more severe at the back of her legs, although the knees were badly bruised.'

'So if she was back up against the parapet,

fighting someone off, her raincoat would ride up . . . I'll tell the scene-of-crime boys to have a look at that bridge. Slim chance, though, with all this bloody rain. It's scarcely stopped since it happened.'

'There could still be traces embedded in the stone.'

Hunter gave this some thought, to the accompaniment of distant whistling sounds. 'You're saying it wasn't an accident?'

'I'm not going on record with that—but we both know it wasn't. By the position and nature of the injuries—this was deliberate. And I'm not a wicked old fart.'

'Yes, you are. Sometimes. This is one of your good days. Thanks, Matthew.'

*   *   *

Collier returned, accompanied by PC George Withers. 'You just caught me, I was on my way in for a community liaison meeting,' George said. A slow-moving man with a down-to-earth manner that made people comfortable, George brought dignity to his uniform, contentment to his human lot; it was no good looking to him for the flash of inspiration, but for sheer tenacity he was unbeatable.

Chatfield was his home ground, just as it was Hunter's: a childhood shared in the same streets, Hunter the gang leader even then, although he was the younger of the two. A

38

pattern was established: Hunter ambitious, striving, achieving; George standing stoically by. Time embedded them in their divergent personalities: Hunter had his seniority, a divorce, an alienated daughter; George, a clutch of children and a devoted wife. Time had embedded them in understanding, too, mutual respect and a quicksilver communication where a nod, a smile, a word, were signposts to an unforgotten landscape. So when Hunter had recounted the substance of his conversation with the pathologist and the information supplied by Mrs Wellbed, a flicker of a smile that crossed George's face was mirrored on his own.

'Beattie Booth?' George worried over the name, shook his head. 'No. And from her photograph she looked like anyone around there. If Friday night was her regular, I wouldn't have come across her. Still, I'll do some asking around. I can see where you're going—she was at Miller's Bridge with this feller and he pushed her over.'

'Someone did, she didn't jump in of her own accord.' Hunter turned an enquiring eye on Collier.

'She was on benefit, but she didn't go into the U.B.O. on Friday to sign on.'

'And we know why. Anything further from Hambling? The eyewitness.'

'Yes. Hambling resident, a Mr Bannon, saw a woman dressed like her walking towards

Miller's Bridge just before nine on the Thursday night.'

'Alone?'

'Alone. He was a bit surprised anyone was out in that weather, he's sure he didn't see another pedestrian anywhere. What it was—he lives near the centre of Hambling and he left home about 8.40 p.m. to drive to the Well Green Methodist chapel to pick up his wife from choir practice. He passed a woman just before he got to the bridge. As they were both going in the same direction he didn't see her face but he noticed her clothes. He collected his wife, stood chatting, so it must have been about 9.30 when he made the return journey. No sign of the woman by then, no sign of anyone.'

'No car conveniently parked? It's exceptionally well-lit at that spot.'

'Nothing. The road's so narrow he'd have remembered if he'd had to pull out around one. There's a small car park and picnic area on the east side of the bridge, much used by courting couples—but if there had been anyone parked there, he wouldn't have seen, even in daylight it's so shielded by trees and bushes you can't see into it.'

'Mmm. She was heading towards the car park, but if she didn't have a rendezvous with someone there she was walking *away* from the town. She couldn't have got back to Chatfield under her own steam going that way—the bus station's on the opposite side of Hambling.'

George said, 'I was there in the summer, evening stroll with the missus. It's rural, but not what you'd call isolated. There are houses on either side of the bridge, and in the lanes leading off it, not many, it's true, and some of them are pretty secluded. Even so . . .'

Hunter nodded yes in agreement with George's unspoken assumption. 'Let's get the Hambling lads started on house to house, just in the immediate vicinity.' He brooded. 'There's too much that doesn't add up in this, isn't there?'

George said, 'Yep.'

Collier made the kind of movement that presages a surge of activity, to be stilled at once by Hunter: 'Don't say it—you want to start playing with your damned instrument. Just wait. I can't treat this as murder until I get the go-ahead from the boss.' He reached for the telephone. 'And it's time I had a word with him.'

CHAPTER FIVE

Headquarters Information Technology department worked through the night, setting up the Holmes terminals in the newly established incident room at Hambling police station. First thing in the morning, Detective

Chief Superintendent Garret drove over to Chatfield. 'A murder in Hambling,' he said, entering Hunter's office. '*Hambling* of all places. And the timing's bloody awful. I mean, why do they always wait till funds are low? You're going to have to wrap this up fairly quickly. Drug squad are quiet at the moment, you can use them.'

'I'll bear that in mind, sir. This is George Withers. I told you yesterday what a good job he's doing this end.'

DCS and constable measured one another with the respect of men at the same stage of service; Garret fully aware that a good area man knew everything—or, if he didn't, had cultivated contacts to provide him with information.

'Right, George. Murder briefing's not till ten and it's only half an hour's drive at most to Hambling. Now, I understand you've got a fair amount of background.'

George wasted no time. The Prince Albert pub, he explained, was the dead woman's stamping ground. She was a Friday night regular; not a heavy drinker, went for the company, a laugh and a natter—habit, really. 'About the beginning of September, Mrs Wellbed's daughter, our Marge, said Beattie started dropping hints about this man she'd met—she didn't say how or where. He took her "somewhere ever so nice". Asked his name—*that'd be telling*, etcetera. Asked why he didn't come in the Prince Albert—*he wouldn't be seen dead in a dump like that.* After a while all this started getting up everyone's nose. The last time she was at the Albert someone accused her of behaving like effing royalty and she said—she'd had a drop more than usual—she'd soon be living like effing royalty. She was going to be in clover, have her own car, live in a posh house. Some sarky bugger said no doubt with a swimming pool and tennis court. She said no, the garden was big enough but she wasn't bothered about things like that.' George paused and looked at Hunter.

'Wild talk, George?'

'I'm reserving judgement for the moment.'

'Fair enough,' Hunter said. George would have his reasons; whatever conclusion he came to would be sound.

'All this wasn't what you'd call a collective discussion—just a few words here and there, with this person or that, or a group sitting at another table. As near as possible I've used her own words. She was getting a lot of barracking; maybe because of that, she hit back. Next week—she said. You'll see, I'll show you buggers. Everything'll be set up then, or arranged. There'll be no backing out. I'll get what's due to me. Various suggestions about what that was. "I won't have to listen to ignorant bastards like you any more. I'll be in my proper station in life. He said it's only what I deserved."'

Garret said, 'Proper station . . . Heroines in Victorian novels say things like that.'

'No, it's not likely to be her usual form of expression,' George said stolidly.

Hunter said, 'She got it from him?'

George nodded. 'He exists, this man. Whoever, wherever, whyever. I think the house does, too, and she's been there. It would have to be with him.'

'I'm with you on that, George,' Hunter said. 'Well done.'

They waited in respectful silence for the few moments it took the DCS to turn the matter over in his mind. 'Yes. Well done, very thorough. You've got to the heart of it— amongst her cronies. The type of woman she was—she just wouldn't have the imagination to dream up something like this. Keep at it. What we need is a description of this man. Somebody must have seen her with him.'

*   *   *

The morning briefing was over by eleven; administrative items dealt with, personnel split into pairs—uniformed men working in plain clothes with an experienced detective constable or sergeant. After thought, Hunter decided it was worth following up Reggie Willoughby's admittedly tenuous connection and assigned James Collier and Woman Detective Constable Annette Jones as the project team to work on Willoughby's habits, inclinations, reputation and alibi—especially his alibi, which was not yet on Holmes. All his verifiable movements put him much too far away at the time of Beattie's death—but someone had taken the trouble to accuse him, he'd put up a distracted performance at his initial interview—although blameless people were known to do that out of terror at being caught in the relentless cogs of the law. And, Hunter had to admit, he would consider anything that had the remotest chance of getting them farther forward.

By evening briefing the investigation had progressed although not exactly, as Hunter put it, at hyper-speed.

At the Chatfield end, DC Moore and PC Hubbard focussed on Beattie's flat, talking to her neighbours, showing her photograph and finally—ascertaining without any doubt that it was hers and empty—breaking in. Dusting revealed her own prints and an assortment that could have been anyone's. As for tangible evidence of an affair—a complete blank. Beattie had no telephone, therefore no personal list of numbers. If she had an address book or diary—and that was considered doubtful—one or both could have been in her handbag—still missing. She had not at any time been seen in the company of a man who was not known to the locality. She dressed herself up and went out . . .

To the Prince Albert. To bingo. To unknown destinations.

To her death.

It was the Bus Station at Chatfield that yielded something positive, confirming Hunter's hunch about Beattie's mode of transport.

'The driver of the number 87 recognised Beattie as the woman he picked up at the Causeway stop on Thursday night,' DC Moore reported.

'And the number 87?' Hunter queried.

'Chatfield to Chester.'

'Calling at Hambling?'

'Yes, guv. He remembered it was Thursday because that was the day the really heavy spell of rain started—it was coming down in buckets so there weren't many people about. She'd made the journey on at least two previous occasions—he thinks also on a Thursday. The first time, a fine evening early September, he noticed her because she was wearing a deep purple track suit, made him think of an over-ripe Victoria plum.'

'A man with imagination. Track suit . . . I don't see her as the aerobic type.'

'It wasn't meant to be functional. He said she was "dressed up" in it—high heels, shiny handbag. She didn't go to Hambling bus station, though. Each time she got off two stops before, at the Peartree turning.'

'There's nothing there,' Hunter said,

thinking. Fields, a few scattered houses, farms, tracks plunging through woods.

'No, well. The driver wondered where she was going to hike off to in her stilettos. So he kept an eye on her in his mirror as he started away. There's an old-type brick bus shelter in the pull-off there. As far as he could tell she stayed in it.'

'Waiting for someone to pick her up.'

'Looks like it.'

Hunter got up to consult the map on the wall. 'That small road at the Peartree turning, leading off from behind the bus shelter. It was the old Hambling road, before the by-pass was built. See, it winds through the outskirts, then turns west into the town proper. But, you see, turning east, there's quite a spread of residential property. And there—just a little over a mile—Miller's Bridge.'

The implications of this caused a surge of speculation:

'The secluded car park, trees, high hawthorn hedges. It could have been their regular courting place—'

'Or one of several—'

'Or they might have been there just that once —'

'Or never—'

'That old road. What's on it?' Hunter turned to DC Hughes. 'Gareth, you're local. Tell us about it.'

'There's nothing on it to speak of. Not too

47

far down, a derelict farm, but nothing else till you get—as you said—to the residential property—and that's pretty sparse at first. That road's hardly used now, except locals. But this man, Mr X, picking her up, he could drive from anywhere round here—in town or round the outskirts. If he was too early, and he waited near the bus shelter, it's all got so overgrown that end of the road the bus driver wouldn't see him from the by-pass.'

'But she would—from the bus shelter.'

'Oh, yes.'

'Right. So we have to find if anyone else did. We can use the local rag—the *Argus*, isn't it? They've been in on this from the start.'

PC Taylor of the Hambling force said, 'They've phoned every day, bit cheesed off we've had nothing for them so far.'

'Well, we'll be back on the front page now it's murder. Local radio—a press release. What we want—did anyone see a car on Thursday night, going up or down that road, parked, waiting, picking a woman up? Ron and Bert—I want you on the 87 bus next Thursday evening—talk to everyone, driver again, passengers, anyone who saw Beattie and might have spoken to her. And I want a road check next Thursday at the same time. O.K?'

DI Graham Hacket asked, 'Are we assuming a scenario: adulterous husband—bit on the side? He makes promises he regrets, tries to pull out. She gets awkward, finishes up in the

48

Chat.'

'A married man puts Willoughby in the clear.'

It was a natural point to turn to Collier and WDC Annette Jones, who had been out on a sortie of discreet enquiries. They worked well together, their attractiveness and good manners a passport to every social level; they had not the slightest erotic interest in each other to impair their efficiency. Hunter harboured a secret, basic lust for Annette, best converted to the admission that she was one of his favourites. If challenged, far from denying this, he would have pointed out that few human creatures could help having as favourite a generously curved 5' 10" with raven hair and a smile of scrupulously controlled impudence.

'Let's start with his alibi. Where have you got with that?' Hunter asked.

'About as far as we can, but that doesn't amount to much,' Collier said. 'In brief, this was his statement. He left home 7.30-ish, drove to Midham (that's about fifteen miles south) to visit his friend Robert Salter who has a market garden outside Midham. Salter wasn't in; his old dad, who lives with him, was also out so there was no one to see Willoughby arrive or leave—but as he was leaving he heard a dog barking. Drove to the Feathers at Midham, where he and Salter are known, stayed about half an hour. Left about 8.30 and drove to the Queen's Arms at Crale, about ten miles south. Stayed there about half an hour—saw some people he knew by sight. On the way back was held up in a traffic queue on the A51 because a lorry had overturned. Arrived at Salter's about quarter to ten. Salter was in by then so they sat talking and drinking coffee and watching telly until about a quarter to twelve. Then he drove home.'

'So. What about the time he *left* home?'

'As he put it—immediately after dinner. His sister—Miss Helen Willoughby—can verify that. We haven't seen her yet. When he arrived at Salter's market garden at Midham—'

'That's the chap who's on one of those gardening programmes on TV, isn't it? Not that I watch them. Yes. When he arrived.'

'He said he heard a dog barking. There's a young couple work for Salter, live in a bungalow on the property. The husband was making his rounds when his dog began to bark and run towards Salter's cottage. When he got there a white Ford Mondeo was disappearing out of the drive. He couldn't read the number but he thought the car was Willoughby's, he's used to seeing him about the place.'

'And the pubs? The Feathers?'

'Yes, the landlord had a word with him—knew him over the years from coming in with Salter—and as *he's* something of a local celebrity everyone recognises him. Same thing at the Queen's Arms at Crale.'

'Mmm. He drove farther and farther south and every bugger saw him. What about this lorry overturning?'

'That checks out with R.T.A. incidents for that day, we can practically tie it down to the minute. The road was blocked for quarter of an hour. Willoughby arrived just as it happened, so he'd be first away, that'd put him at Midham 9.45.'

'Our eye-witness—Mr Bannon?—what time did he see Beattie?'

'He saw her approaching Miller's Bridge just before nine. As you said, guv, Willoughby was just too far away. Quarter to till quarter past nine he was at the Queens Arms, twenty-five miles away. The estimated time of death is 9.30. He just couldn't have been at the scene to do her in, then get back to Salter's by 9.45.'

'You're satisfied Salter is telling the truth?'

Annette said, 'Oh, yes. We had a long interview with him, he was helpful, very concerned. He and Reggie have been friends for years, they were at Hambling Grammar together. Salter is very worried about the effect all this is having on Reggie, and he's adamant he's incapable of harming anyone. I'd say Salter's a good friend. He was very open, nothing evasive or cagey, perfectly willing to talk about Reggie and the "nice gels" he took out from time to time. He did get a bit embarrassed trying *not* to say that a woman

51

dressed up in all that plastic couldn't possibly be Reggie's type. I don't know. Reggie might have his girlfriends and maybe boyfriends, too, but . . .' Annette hesitated. 'I got the strong impression he's one of those asexual beings.'

'Like Bertie Wooster?' Hunter asked, purely for the pleasure of watching her gulp back a yell of laughter. 'I think it's time I had a word with this perpetual juvenile of doubtful gender.'

Collier said, 'I'm afraid you can't at the moment, guv. He's gone away, short holiday. Apparently there was unpleasantness in the town and at his office—at least, that was how he saw it. We spoke to his boss—he said people were really being quite decent but inclined to make jokes and Willoughby was getting into a nervous state. He turned in a sick note and has gone to stay with a relative in Cheltenham.'

'Where else?' Hunter sighed. 'Oh, well, it'll keep.'

A question from DC Powell. 'Guv, you haven't released her name yet.

'No. Right. According to Mrs Wellbed—who's our only source of information on Beattie to date—there's a cousin called Muriel who's shacked up with a guy in Newcastle. We've had the Newcastle police on to it today but so far they've not traced her. She might have moved on. I'm giving it till tomorrow then I'll give her name in our daily press release. Someone might come forward with more information. Right. Anything else?'

He looked at them all, then at his watch. 'We don't know how long this is going to run, we've got to pace ourselves, I don't want anyone burning out. The most practical thing I can say at the moment is that the Frog and Nightgown's been open for two and half hours and I'm dying of thirst. Who's for or against?'

CHAPTER SIX

A telephone message from Paula on Thursday was passed on to Liz. Unavailable to take the call, she caught its flying fragments. Urgent . . . *must* see you as soon as . . . *vital* . . .

Her first thought was for Helen. She phoned but there was no answer. Requesting Friday afternoon off, she skipped lunch and drove to Hambling, straight to Helen's.

No one answered the front door. Quelling a flutter of alarm, she kept trying, then retreated from the porch to stand looking at the house.

It was impossible to get into Woodside unless someone opened the front door. The long double frontage, set back to the left with Helen's garage built on, ended at a stout twelve foot fence to the adjoining property. To the right: a wrought iron gate in a high stone wall; Reggie's garage flush against next door's tall, impenetrable hedge.

During the day, when people were about, the iron gate was unlocked, the fact that it was now locked indicated there was no one at home—and yet, drifting from beyond the house came the acrid smell of woodsmoke. Old George, the jobbing gardener, would be in the far reaches of the back garden, not able to hear even if she called. Why he should want to lock himself in she couldn't imagine.

Where was Helen? Had anything happened to her? Had Paula's call substance after all? There was only one thing to do—attack from the rear.

Leaving her car in the drive, she walked quickly out of the front gate and trotted along the path through the spinneys and clearing that fronted the houses. Three houses along, she turned left down a footpath. Here, she was on the labyrinth of paths, bridleways and tracks that circled Hambling as far as her own house. They were bounded by walls, fences, dense hedges and massive old trees. Some of the paths were so narrow the trees met overhead, forming tunnels, fragrant with honeysuckle on summer evenings; in the snow, luminous, magic caverns.

Her trot quickened to a jog. Puddles, fallen leaves, hoofprints, bicycle tracks—she squelched through them, covering the ground rapidly until she reached the dense shrubs and tangled briars that guarded the end of Helen's garden. There was a gap—so overgrown it was invisible to passers-by, but she knew it, plunged in. Thorns raked her clothes, wet leaves slapped her face. After a momentary struggle she was at a high, solid fence. There was a door in it—like the gap, camouflaged from the gaze of strangers, but Liz knew it was there and how to deal with it.

She hopped on to the base of a lopped tree, grasped a fence post and heaved herself up. Hanging by one arm she performed the shoulder-dislocating exercise of reaching over the top of the door with the other hand and drawing back the bolt. Letting herself down on to the tree stump again, she levered the upper half of the door back, squeezed her hand through and worked the lower bolt free.

There were more shrubs to be negotiated before she reached the vegetable garden; sprinting, she burst through an opening in the trellis to a cleared space. Helen—not old George—wielding a fork, energetically turned a bonfire. She took a step back, squeaked, '*Liz!*'

'Helen—' Liz, panting, put her hand out in a calming gesture.

'What is it?' Helen looked round wildly, holding the fork as a weapon.

'I'm sorry, I—'

'What on *earth* are you doing?'

'You didn't answer the door. I smelt the

bonfire . . . I thought . . . you see, Paula rang and . . .'

A hiatus, as if they were two strangers colliding in a crowded street—then a confusion of apologies, explanations. Liz with twigs in her hair, Helen pulling herself together. After a while, they were laughing at the silliness of it.

Helen said, 'You haven't forgotten the old trick with the back gate that Reggie taught you. I hope you've shut it.'

'Oh, God—' Liz hurtled back the way she had come. Returned. 'Reggie—how is he? Only, you see, Paula's message . . . *Urgent. Vital.* Well, I thought it might be to do with him.'

'There's nothing vital and she shouldn't have bothered you. Really. He's perfectly all right, still in Cheltenham. So you came rushing up here, bursting in . . . Liz, you're a sight.'

'And an ass. Look, let me help—you shouldn't be doing this. Where's old George?'

'He has so many jobs to catch up on with other people, this is the first decent day since all that rain. No, really, I can manage. I've got myself organised.'

She had used newspaper to start the fire, a pile of it stood nearby with a can of petrol. The fire looked as if it had been burning reluctantly for some time. Garden rubbish mingled with household waste: bundles and boxes, their contents distorted and blackened. Shoes, straps and buckles half consumed, bundles of

56

cloth, rolls of old wallpaper . . . clouds of eye-stinging smoke.

Liz said, 'You shouldn't be heaving all this stuff about.'

'Well, so much was due to go to the tip, but as Reggie's not been here to take it, and I couldn't ask George, he does so resent anything beyond what he calls his parameters—so the only thing is to burn it.'

'But struggling out here.'

'Where else?' Helen said rather shortly. In the house, she had long ago had every grate taken out, keeping the beautiful Edwardian surrounds as settings for gas fires that brought the comfort of flickering flames to every downstairs room—but left nowhere to burn anything.

'Yes, I'm sorry,' Liz murmured. Now that she had time to consider, she was disturbed by Helen's appearance: the dark-socketed eyes told of sleeplessness; a deep V drew the fine brows together in irritation or anxiety.

Obviously, she was feeling Reggie's absence more than she would admit, and, in this case, compensating by physical exertion. Liz knew about displacement activity; when she was thoroughly fed-up or angry, she cleaned her house like a fury.

'But, Liz, what are you doing here now? It's much too early for you.' When Liz said she had the afternoon off, Helen said, 'You mean you took it off to come and see if I was all right. And you must have missed lunch.'

'Well . . .'

'You're a very naughty girl. Go in the house at once, clean yourself up and make us both a cup of tea. By the time you've done that I shall be finished here and I shall organise you something to eat.'

'Let me just help—' she went to take the fork.

Helen wrested it back with surprising force. 'Go along. At once.'

Liz went meekly.

In the kitchen, the breakfast bay was set into a window that looked on to Helen's daintily plotted herb garden. Sitting there, Liz finished off an excellent omelette and brown bread. She had cleaned herself up, her filthy shoes were drying in the porch; Helen had put her into a pair of Reggie's golfing socks to keep her feet warm.

'Now tell me about Reggie.'

'I phone him every day, he's sounding much more himself.'

'When is he coming home?'

'Ah, that I don't know. And I'm not going to press him. I don't want him to come home before he's ready and not be able to cope with any setbacks.'

'Setbacks? You mean . . . gossip, rumours,' Liz said warily, prompted to unwilling recollection of her previous weekend in Hambling. After she had left Helen—

shopping, going about her errands, passing time in ordinary ways that delighted her—she had become aware of odd comments, even odder looks. She tried to tell herself she was being over-sensitive, but she knew that was not true. Some people, pressing close, emitted curiosity like a smell. Others, scarcely known, became effusive, beginning rapid, embarrassed monologues about anything; eyes met hers with diffidence, refused to meet hers at all. Afterwards, alone at home, she astonished herself by a bout of angry tears—on Reggie's behalf, she thought, but for herself, too, because there was no challenge to meet, nowhere for her defensiveness to go except in uneasiness and scorn.

She had made a resolution to keep the least hint of this from Helen, only to be relieved of her anxiety by Helen saying, 'I know the whole town was buzzing with the affair—but people have awfully short memories and I'm sure it's all died down—or very nearly. No, I don't think Reggie's in danger of being upset by anything like that. No, it's Paula.'

Liz gave a muted groan.

'She says I'm being unrealistic. I say she's being . . . Well, let me explain, then you can tell me what you think. You know she went to the Warners for their silver wedding. Bess Warner phoned me on the Monday to say they were all very sorry about Reggie—etcetera. I played it down, of course, but I was most

59

annoyed with Paula, I really don't want her chattering the length and breadth of England about our concerns, it's too bad. I had no intention of making an issue of it so I didn't even mention Bess had rung when I next saw Paula. But she made a dreadful fuss when she discovered Reggie was in Cheltenham—she didn't know anything about his being away.'

'No, of course, she left terribly early last Saturday morning and you and Reggie hadn't decided he'd go to Uncle William till later. But why on earth should she make a fuss?'

'Because Reggie had gone away without informing the police.'

Liz stared. 'But—why should he?'

'Why indeed? She says the police always need to know the whereabouts of a suspect—'

Suspect . . . The word would not come out, for which Liz was thankful because she would have shouted it and Helen needed reassurance, not a lot of noise. She was so angry she could only say, 'Let me count to ten.'

'I'll join you. One, two . . .'

They counted together. Helen sighed. Liz said briskly, 'Reggie isn't a suspect. She's being ridiculous. *That's* what her potty phone call was about.'

'My fault. I refused to listen, I told her not to talk nonsense. I never imagined she would pester you at school. I did think she might try to get hold of Reggie—so I telephoned Uncle William and told him to say that Reggie was out if she phoned.'

'Good.' Liz thought it over. 'That's what you meant by setbacks.'

'Yes. It's so unnecessary, and it could upset Reggie—just for some bee she's got in her bonnet. She says I'm shielding him—and deceiving myself about the reality of the situation.'

'Paula doesn't care about reality, she cares about meddling. I'll talk to her.'

'Oh, darling, would you? I'd be so grateful. I'm heartily sick of arguing with her.'

Liz considered Helen; with the relaxation of tension her face had become pale and worn. 'That's why you didn't answer when I phoned—why you took yourself off to the end of the garden. You were hiding.'

Helen looked sheepish.

'I certainly will go and see her. Now.' Liz paused, thought. 'No, tomorrow. She'll know I've seen you. If I go rushing off to her she'll think she's got us both in a panic. Tomorrow. Ummm, supposing she phones this evening. Or comes round here.'

'She very well could.'

'We—ell . . . I know, we'll go out—have dinner somewhere. Then she won't know where we are.'

'What a nice idea. My treat. Yes, I insist. What fun—we can both hide—and have a jolly nice time while we're about it.' Helen's smile had a glint of mischief.

'Oh, Helen, that's better. You were so on edge. You must put your mind at rest—she's absolutely wrong. And how dare she call Reggie a suspect.'

'She did apologise, said it was an expression she used without thinking. She really was sorry. And she does try to help. One must make allowances.'

'Why?' Liz asked balefully.

'I've tried to explain before. About the way it always affected her—being sent away so young.'

'How could it have been helped? You couldn't—'

'I know, it was unavoidable. Father wouldn't have been . . . There was never any kindness in this house, Liz. She was much better off, growing up with other children, having a happy family life. But she's always felt—pushed out. She's never said so, she would regard it as disloyalty to the Warners, but it's there. That's why she's so . . .'

'Rebarbative is the word you're looking for, I think.'

'Unkind,' Helen reproved softly.

'But true.'

Helen did not argue.

CHAPTER SEVEN

Liz thought she loved Hambling so much because her hold on it had always been precarious. Her restless, unhappy mother, moving house so many times during and in the intervals of two deserting husbands, had taken her backwards and forwards, in and out. She swore she spent her childhood watching Hambling recede through the window of a bus, a car, a train, knowing fragile friendships lost, knowing the familiar would use her absence to rework itself into the strange.

She was never sure whether she loved the place for itself, because it was enchanting, or because it meant Helen and Reggie. They stood in place of a family for her. She had never known her father, being only a year old when he absconded; there had been a stepfather of brief duration who hadn't wanted her. Her mother died when she was in her last year at university; by then, her loyalties were entrenched. She had the most insecure recollection of Helen's wispy and ailing mother. A long and complicated memory of ruses, fibs and fast footwork that kept her out of the terrifying old man Willoughby's way. And what could only be regarded as a series of mental collisions that characterised her relationship with Paula. Paula always bullied her. There was nothing personal in it—Paula, with the maniacal assertion of the righteous, bullied everyone. The trick was to develop defences. Rather to her surprise, Liz, grown up, discovered she had, although they weren't always reliable and in times of stress diminished to the simple urge to pick up the nearest heavy object and fell Paula with it.

On a Saturday morning Paula would not be at her office. She had a computer software business in Hambling, originally with a partner. There had once been talk of expanding, opening another office in Chatfield, but the partnership had broken up, with the acrimony inseparable from all Paula's doings. The partner moved to Chatfield. Paula stayed on in Hambling, retaining the marital home as part of her divorce settlement.

It stood in a shrubberied square of handsome houses with front gardens neat behind ornate iron railings. Paula—despising the middle-class attitudes of her neighbours, their endless striving to repair, restore—insisted her house proclaim its honest-to-God simplicity. It did this with faded paint, ill-fitting curtains and—a new addition that appalled Liz—the front garden full of piles of bricks, clearly visible to passers-by. The spacious porch was a lumber room of cardboard boxes and bin liners stuffed full of clothing for jumble sales, refugees, anyone Paula could find unfortunate enough to require them. A small gate and path, once used by servants and tradespeople, led round to the side door, which was reached through a long glass porch. This was stacked with fridges, washing machines, tables, chairs, bundles of bedding and curtaining, rolls of carpet—all waiting to be passed on to the deserving. Eventually.

Determined not to throw herself into whatever part Paula had scripted for her, Liz said by way of greeting, 'Paula, what on earth are all those bricks in the front garden? Are you going to have some work done?'

'Oh, those. They're from the old property that's being demolished behind the Fire Station. Charlie Willis bought them, to make ornamental brick paths in their new garden.'

'But they haven't moved yet.'

'No, that's the trouble. He's nowhere to put them, so I said I'd store them for him.'

It was typical of Paula, her kindness and wrong-headedness. It would be a waste of time to point out to her that in doing a favour for a friend she had made her garden look like a tip and probably enraged her neighbours. She did so much for other people she often got into terrible muddles and became upset when anyone criticised her. It was true there were times when it was difficult to tell where kindness ended and meddling began.

The kitchen was old fashioned, high ceilinged, the walls emulsioned in rectangles

65

and triangles of orange, purple and green; the open shelves were crammed with utensils, pans, crockery; the Aga was always, mysteriously, not working. Paula made something tasteless called coffee in large, chipped mugs and sat down at the cluttered table with Liz. She had a short, thick, restless body, a plump face on which there was always a searching expression, and beautiful chestnut hair forever spilling out of clips and combs.

'Now listen, this is serious, Liz. For Christ's sake I tried and tried to get you last night. Do you know, do you *know* Reggie's done a runner?'

Very deliberately, Liz said, 'Paula, if you don't stop this histrionic rubbish I'll get up and walk out. Reggie is staying with Uncle William in Cheltenham. He couldn't be more visible. Or anywhere more respectable.'

Paula regarded her without speaking, her face grave and knowing. At last, she said, 'Ah, yes. I should have realised. Helen's got at you.'

'Helen does not "get at" anyone.' Liz felt her teeth gritting.

'You were with her last night and she insisted everything's perfectly normal. Don't say it is, Liz, because much as you want to play her game you can't pretend nothing's happened. Somehow, desperately unjust as it is, Reggie's been linked with this dead woman and everyone's talking about it. He's on the verge of a breakdown. And he has run away, hasn't he? He always does. He's never been in a mess like this before, but other things, stupid money things, getting in the wrong sort of company—somehow he's always managed to leave it to Helen to clear up the mess. And she has. But this time it's different and it's come really close to her.'

'Yes,' Liz said unhappily, thinking of the Helen of yesterday, the woman exhausted with overstrained nerves. She sat silent beneath Paula's gaze. Oh, God, what else is she going to say that's got too much truth in it?

'She protects him, and she needs him, too. You know and I know they live in a cocoon. Left-overs from the 1930s. What single, sensible notion have either of them got between them for dealing with 1990?'

'I think you're exaggerating a bit—'

Paula made an exasperated noise. 'Of course you think I'm exaggerating—that's because you're as bad as they are half the time. You encourage them in all these outworn notions of gentility and reputation and—'

'Hang on, hang on. I respect the way they choose to live their lives. I don't encourage them to ignore reality.'

'They don't need any bloody encouragement. And yes, you do.'

'How, for God's sake?'

Paula's long-drawn out 'We—ell . . .' made it so obvious she was casting about that Liz was on the point of saying *See*—regrettably aware they were behaving like two small girls in a playground—when Paula said, 'All that business in the summer with Wilfred Heatherington.'

Taken by surprise, Liz concealed—she hoped—her awkwardness. 'There wasn't any "business" with Helen and—'

'Exactly. Exactly. There *might* have been if you'd just left them to get on with it—'

'They had no intention of getting on—'

'But no, you were always hanging around—you and Reggie "making up foursomes" but *he* just does what anyone tells him to do, anyway. Oh, come on, admit it. You can't accept—you're just plain embarrassed at the thought of a woman of Helen's age having a sexually fulfilling relationship with a man—a man of his age, too. You think it's not quaite naice—'

'Don't tell me what I think, Paula. I'll tell you any embarrassment I feel is this prying into something so personal—'

Paula smiled her pinched, patronising smile. '*So* mealymouthed. Are you trying to tell me you didn't influence Helen?'

'Of course I didn't influence her. I wouldn't dream of speaking to her on the subject. And if I remember, Paula, you had a great deal to say against Wilfred. He was an adventurer—after the Willoughby money—'

'Somebody had to protect Helen's interests. I had to make sure. No one knew anything about him.'

68

'Oh, for God's sake, loads of people know all about Wilfred—he lived here once, years ago. He's still got friends all over the place. His daughter's lived all her married life over near Tatton Park. He's got more than enough of his own to buy and sell Woodside'—a wild overestimate, but Liz was heading for incoherence, so badly did she want to drop the subject. Paula persisted in old arguments. She could keep them going for months, years, long after everyone had forgotten what they were about. This was one of her favourites; from time to time she accused Liz of all sorts of things—never of what really happened, because, of course, she didn't know; but she had the tenacity to hang on until she found out *something*. Anything. Or made it up.

'I have to go to the loo,' Liz said. Only by physically removing herself could she stop Paula staring into her face so intently.

She made for the downstairs cloakroom. The house smelt sour, the lavatory smelt worse. She found she actually wanted to pee— anger, or guilt, had been at work on her bladder.

Wilfred. Sexy, gallant Wilfred. No one knew . . . 'Liz, dear girl, I shall have to leave. Go home. There's some talk starting, people are putting the wrong construction on this. I couldn't bear Helen to be hurt or embarrassed.'

'I know what you mean—it's all right now,

but if you stay much longer . . . We'll all miss you. Have you—have you got someone in Hampshire? Oh, I shouldn't ask that, should I?'

'Why not? The answer's no, anyway. Delightful as she is, much as I admire and respect her, it isn't Helen I'm lusting after. It's you, Liz.'

A furious inner response: excitement and alarm. *He's seventy. He's adorable. I wonder what it would be like . . . This is dreadful, I would never, never hurt Helen.* She said all the right things; he agreed they were right, wistfully. Amongst his goodbye presents to them all—a beautiful double string of pearls for Liz.

She went briskly back to the kitchen, rinsing her hands under the tap, wondering absently how even Paula managed to accumulate so much washing up. 'Paula, God knows how we got sidetracked on to this—it's just a silly waste of time. Let's get back to where we started.'

'About them being so unworldly. It's up to *us. We* have to stand between them and the nasty old world.' Paula did not regard this in any way incompatible with her assertion that by doing exactly that, Liz had interfered, irretrievably, with Helen's happiness. Liz almost screamed aloud.

'Well, I have to agree, they're not awfully well-equipped . . . What I was thinking—if I go along with what Helen wants, it'll comfort her to think eventually everything will be all right. I don't know what else to do, Paula.'

'No, I don't, either,' Paula murmured, making Liz stare in surprise. It was unthinkable—Paula without an instant solution. 'Look, mightn't it have been better, really, if Reggie had told the police he was going away?'

'Why on earth should he? He doesn't have to report his movements, he's not a suspect. They just questioned him that once and they haven't bothered since. Just to eliminate him from their enquiries.'

Paula squawked with unamused laughter. 'But why? They *never gave a reason.* They should have told him why they found it necessary to question him. Helen doesn't know, does she?'

'No. Well, she thinks somehow they had a reason to believe he was in the area at the relevant time and they wanted to find out if he'd seen anyone—'

'Oh, come off it. He was nowhere *near* Miller's Bridge that night. We've gone over his movements *ad nauseam,* haven't we?'

'Yes,' Liz said miserably. 'I must admit, I have wondered *why* they picked on him.'

'We ought to know, as his family. *He* should be told. And there's something else, something you and Helen don't know.'

'What?'

Paula made a uncharacteristically helpless

gesture. 'You said, a minute ago, that they haven't bothered since they got him to make that statement.'

'Well? Well—they haven't,' Liz said almost angrily. 'They haven't asked to see him or—or anything.'

'No.'

'So?'

Paula shrugged, as if agreeing, then shook her head—a silent pantomime that took some time. Eventually, she said, 'But they've been asking questions about him. All over the place.'

Liz leaned forward, forcing herself not to come up on cue with the reaction Paula's sense of drama required. And helpless against the knowledge: she's not acting. This is serious. 'Just—explain,' she said slowly.

She had to wait. Paula stirred her coffee, slowly, held some kind of inward communion. At last she said, 'All over the place. Questions.'

'Where? Who?'

'Well . . .' Paula thought for some time, brows drawn down. 'Robert at Midham, for one.'

'Why?' Liz asked, after waiting for Paula to continue.

'Why?' Paula made a helpless face. 'Who knows?'

'Let's start with the easy bit. How do *you* know?'

'That's it, you see. Sheer chance.'

'*What* chance?'

'What? Oh—yes. I drove Charlie and Linette Willis over there the other day, their car's having its gearbox fixed or something and they want some ideas on garden design when they move—you know they're getting a house in that new development . . .'

Liz swallowed the urge to yell *Sod the Willis's*, gripped her coffee mug and waited.

'. . . anyway, that was when Robert told me the police had been there, asking all sorts of questions about Reggie. They'd even been to the pubs Reggie and Robert go to. And they talked to that couple who work for Robert.'

'*I* know,' Liz interrupted, excited, relieved. 'Of course. The statement he made—they couldn't just accept it at face value. They had to check it. Those were all the places he went—you know—that night . . .'

But Paula was shaking her head solemnly from side to side. 'No, you're not thinking straight. They checked his alibi over a week ago. This is the second time around. Robert was pretty upset. He's spoken up loyally for Reggie—naturally, it's what one would do for a friend. The last thing he expected was the police back on his doorstep. After all, Reggie's a private individual, but Robert is high profile, he has his television image to consider. It won't do him any good to have all the gossip starting up all over again.'

'Well, that's more or less guaranteed if you went into all this with the Willis's drinking in

73

every word. Good God, you know what they are.'

Paula put up a restraining hand. 'Liz, you're so impetuous, wait, listen. Don't take this as gospel—although as things are it could very well be true . . .'

She said nothing more until Liz asked wearily, 'What could?'

'I've heard they've been to his office.'

'But—why?'

'I'll tell you what I think. I think they haven't a bloody clue what they're about and they'll pick on anyone just to look as if they're getting somewhere. There have been miscarriages of justice. Perfectly innocent people have gone to—'

'Shut up,' Liz said savagely. 'Shut up, Paula.'

'Oh, Liz, I'm sorry—I'm sorry. Don't be upset. It's just that I've got more experience than you about how rotten the world can be. You have to admit you do have a pretty sheltered life, shut away in your ivory tower without the responsibility of a husband and kids.'

Liz wondered how her personal circumstances had become relevant. Her head felt bludgeoned, she sat very still, threatened by the conviction that everything in this hectic room was about to topple over and submerge her. She had to get out. She had to do something. She had to protect Reggie. And Helen.

74

'*Now* you can see,' Paula said, 'why I got in a bit of a flap about Reggie going off without telling the police. I'm not at all sure—as they *seem* still be carrying on their enquiries—if there's not some obligation on him to let them know where he is. Or, maybe, Helen should have told them.'

'*What!*'

'Well, you just don't know how they think. If she appears to be colluding in some way—I mean, of course, she's *not*—but she has no idea all this is going on. I mean, if they're questioning other people, mightn't they question her—'

'But they have no *reason* to.'

'How do we know? How do we know what sort of a case they're concocting?'

'We'll find out. I'll find out. I'm fed up with all this.' Liz stood up, hoisted her handbag. 'I'll bloody well go and ask them.'

Paula regarded her with astonishment, then admiration. 'Oh, Liz, I think that's absolutely the right thing to do.'

Liz was on the move, wrenching open the side door, flinging herself into the conservatory and colliding with an errant sideboard. With an anxiety so uncharacteristic she appeared to be wringing her hands, Paula followed. 'Try and calm down, they'll just browbeat you if you're upset . . . And come back afterwards and let me know.'

'Browbeat. Browbeat. No bugger's going to

browbeat me,' Liz muttered, flailing her way through the obstacle course of the porch.

CHAPTER EIGHT

The weather made her feel worse, setting her teeth on edge. A theatrical day, lowering banks of cloud splitting open in purple rimmed glares of sunlight. In the centre of town she drove round the church green to the frenzy of Saturday morning wedding bells. The glittering light fled, rain came down in a curtain, she almost skidded on a drift of sodden leaves.

By the time she reached the police station the downpour was over; she skipped shining puddles, rushing gutters. Somewhere inside her head a voice said *I must calm down*. She didn't listen to it but she did manage to stop herself grabbing the first person she came upon in the entrance hall of the police station—a uniformed constable much shorter that herself. 'This is where you have the incident room, isn't it? The Miller's Bridge business. I insist on seeing someone in authority. Don't tell me no one's available, I won't go away till I see someone.'

'I think I'll do,' a voice said pleasantly behind her. Registering only that the man was big enough to fill the doorway in which he stood, Liz strode past him into an office. He followed. 'I'm Chief Inspector Hunter. Please sit down.'

'My uncle, Reggie Willoughby.' She spoke unthinkingly. Of course, Reggie and Helen were not her uncle and aunt, but that was what she had called them from childhood, had to school herself to stop doing it. In absent-minded or—in this case—fraught moments, she jettisoned accuracy.

'Yes?'

What sort of a life did anyone live who could use a single word like a brick wall? 'You know perfectly well why I'm here. You're victimising him. You owe it to his family to explain why, without the slightest reason, you contacted him in the first place.'

'I don't have to explain anything to you,' Hunter said politely. 'I don't know who you are.'

'Yes, you do. I just told you,' Liz almost shouted.

'I know what you've told me, but how do I know it's true? You could be anyone. A reporter after information. A nosey neighbour. A deranged woman who makes a habit of hurling herself into police stations. You could be—'

'Oh, all *right*—' Liz upended her handbag, scattering its contents over the desk. 'Look—here. Look, a letter from my bank.'

Hunter studied it. 'Yes. It tells me you're Elizabeth Farrell and you live at 42 Bellfield. It

77

doesn't tell me you're related to Reggie Willoughby.'

'What? Oh . . .' Liz opened her wallet. Credit cards, library ticket, RAC membership . . . Confirmation of identity, not relationship. She hunted, feeling stupid. 'No. I see. I don't think there's anything here, um . . .'

'Or here. Interesting as it all is,' Hunter said, studying his littered desk.

Oh, God. She swept everything back into her bag. She daren't look. Tampax. Condoms. Oh, God. 'Look, you'll just have to take my word for now—you can check up as much as you like later. I suppose this is your technique for getting rid of me. Well, I'm not going. You can push Reggie around because he's too weak to stand up for himself—'

'Why should I want to?'

'Don't ask me! I came here for some answers and all you do is sit there and ask questions, you cool bastard.' She heard the last three words suddenly, outside her head, as if someone else had shouted them. She gulped. 'I'm sorry. I really shouldn't have said that, it was unpardonably rude.'

'Don't apologise, we're used to being insulted by members of the public.'

'I deserve that. I'm making an awful mess of this, aren't I?'

'I don't know. How do you usually go about things?'

A visible effort at calm. 'I have to make you

78

understand what a nightmare this is for my uncle and aunt. And it goes on. It was bad enough to question him in the first place. Now you've questioned his friends, and people he scarcely knows. You've even been to his office.'

'How do you know that?'

A rapid mental backtrack. Paula saying *Don't take this as gospel.* But wasn't that bad enough, for God's sake. Rumours everywhere. 'Can you imagine how humiliating that is for him. Policemen marching in—'

'Miss Farrell, my team are professionals, they don't march anywhere drawing attention to people and embarrassing them. How do you know they went to his office?'

She began to have a feeling of menace, untraceable to anything in his attitude. Where did it come from then? Could he influence the air around him? What had Paula said about being browbeaten? Paula had to be bloody right again. 'You don't deny it—'

'I have no reason to. I have every reason to be discreet. Detective Sergeant Collier and Woman Police Constable Jones called at your uncle's office. If you wish, I'll introduce you to them and they'll tell you how they conducted the interview. They revealed their professional status to Mr Willougby's superior—let's see, what's his name? Mr Darrow. To Mr Darrow and no one else, explained that it was necessary for them to fill in some background details on Mr Willoughby in order to eliminate him from their enquiries. *Nothing* they did could have given rise to gossip or speculation about their visit. So. Where did you hear of it?'

'Um. Paula—Reggie's younger sister—'

'That's not the one he lives with?'

'No, that's Helen . . .'

While Liz briefly explained Paula, Hunter studied her. She was looking increasingly unhappy—not merely because she'd made a fool of herself but because—yes—she was genuinely distressed. The sun dazzled through the office window, making her blink. Her eyes were hazel, with splinters of gold. She wore a fringed jacket of supple leather, the colour of antique parchment; an apricot silk shirt. Her short hair had the shallowest of waves, corn-bright. He thought he had never seen a woman so—golden. 'And where did Mrs Pilling get her information?'

'Gossip, not information. She hears everything. I'm pretty sure I can guess how it started.' Liz had had time to think. 'Darrow—Reggie's boss. He's a spiteful old woman, loves a scandal. He wouldn't have been able to keep quiet. I apologise again. Look, could we pretend I've just come in?'

Somewhere, an amused response. She had never encountered anyone who invited confidence and remained so inscrutable. Perhaps it was part of police training.

'How is it Mrs Pilling hears everything and

you don't? Don't you gossip, Miss Farrell?'

'Like blazes, given the chance. It's just that most of the time I'm not around to hear anything . . .' She told him about her job, her weekly commuting.

'So you only see your aunt and uncle at weekends?'

'Yes. But we've always been very close.'

He looked at her consideringly. 'That's why you're here. You want to protect them. Aren't they capable of protecting themselves?'

'No, you see—that's it. They're not. They live in their own world, where everything's gentle and polite and beautifully ordered—the way it was thirty years ago. Look—this isn't fair—I've told you about me and Paula and—Reggie's boss—and everything. You haven't told me a single thing.'

He gave a slight smile, charming, easy; leaned forward. 'Does the name Beattie Booth mean anything to you?'

The question took her by surprise. She sat thoughtfully, then shook her head. After a momentary pause her expression registered. 'Oh . . . Is that . . . Was that . . . You've found out who she was, that poor woman.

'Yes. She lived in Chatfield'—he doubted the name Causeway would mean anything to her—'in one of the tower blocks.' She sat for a while, politely at a loss. 'Has your uncle ever mentioned her to you—have you heard him speak of her to anyone else?'

'No, never. I don't mean to be . . . Well, her description . . . And she lived in Chatfield. Reggie just doesn't know anyone like that.'

'Can you be sure? He goes to Chatfield from time to time, doesn't he? Whereabouts?'

She thought. 'The Conservative Club. One or two night clubs where he can gamble a little with his friends—they think they're terribly laddish but it's all completely harmless.'

'Which clubs?'

'The Manhattan. Merlin's Place.'

He nodded with mild interest. It never occurred to her he was taking notes inside his head. 'Where else?'

She appeared to be about to ask *Does it matter?* but changed her mind. 'Mmm. Sometimes he takes Helen—or a party of them go—to the theatre. Greyhound racing—I went with him once, it was rather fun. Shopping, but only very occasionally. They have an account at Barker's but they prefer to go to Chester.'

'You see. Think about this. There are women who take tickets at doors. Barmaids, waitresses; women who show people to seats, serve in kiosks, sell cigarettes and papers in newsagents. You dismissed it out of hand, the idea he could even have met her. But it isn't impossible, is it?'

'No. I see what you mean. But . . . *met.* That's not knowing, is it? In the sense of a friendship, a relationship. I understand what you're getting at but, really—' her voice had a delicately scathing edge. 'Do you mean you tied Reggie into this on the basis of—of usherettes? Shop assistants he *might* have come across? Wouldn't you say that was rather tenuous?'

'Those were possibilities we had to consider after the phone call.'

'Phone call?'

'Immediately after the announcement of the discovery of the body, we received an anonymous phone call connecting your uncle with the incident.'

He watched her eyes cloud. 'But that's . . . You mean actually *accusing* him? What did they say?'

'That I can't tell you. Only that the caller gave us your uncle's name and said he lived in Hambling.'

'But you *know*—now—don't you? He couldn't have had anything to do with it. He was nowhere near Miller's Bridge that night.'

'True. But that doesn't mean she wasn't known to him. We had to pursue it.

'But couldn't you have started the other way round, so to speak. I mean, you can trace calls, can't you?'

'Only if the station has the facility to record them. Chatfield doesn't.'

'Oh, I see. Did you tell Reggie about it?'

'No. We weren't obliged to. Do you think it would have made any difference?'

She thought only for an instant. 'No. It

wouldn't, he'd have been even more devastated. Helen doesn't have to know, does she? There's nothing to be gained by telling her. I won't. And I'm certainly not going to tell Paula. She'd love something like that, insist on talking it over to "clear the air".'

'Mightn't there be some sense in that? Miss Willoughby is closest to her brother, she might know if someone has a grudge against him. It's not unknown for people to have enemies.'

'Well, in Reggie's case that hardly applies. He really doesn't have a character strong enough to provoke anything more than mild irritation.'

Hunter raised his eyebrows.

'Look—he's generous and kind and sweet natured. I love him, but I'm not blind to his faults. He can be maddeningly dense. Just not getting the point. When—'

She had almost said it. Almost. Because she was ill at ease, had made a fool of herself, felt awkward about being rude.

'Yes?'

'Oh, um—'The meetings at her house. Some silliness. Nothing, nothing to do with the dead woman. *No one's* business except hers and Reggie's. 'Well . . . when he was questioned, for instance. He couldn't see how he was making things worse for himself . . .'

No. Her eyes refusing to meet his, the sudden tension in her body. No, that was not what she had been about to say. 'Miss Farrell, if you know anything—'

—and it was already all over. That Thursday night, he'd had no date with Ms Whoever. He'd been at the other side of Cheshire. 'What could I possibly know? That poor woman means nothing to me, I'd never even heard her name till ten minutes ago. I can assure you, positively, that Reggie never mentioned her. Why should he? I'm convinced he never even knew of her existence. Goodness, is that the time? I must dash.' She stood up, gracefully precipitant, handbag on her shoulder.

'Miss Farrell—' it was a note of warning.

'You can't keep me here, can you?' she asked with an interest so detached, so gracious, that just for an instant she got the better of him.

'Er—no.'

'Good. Then I really must go. I apologise for coming in here like a volcano. Good morning.'

*   *   *

DS Collier came upon Hunter standing in the corridor looking through the window on to a side road of parked cars.

Hunter said, 'Those early Bette Davis films. The way she walked.'

Collier, wondering if he might have a place in the conversation, looked out of the window for help. He saw a golden-haired young woman, head up, striding into a stage set of mulberry clouds dazzled by silver. She wore slim trousers, cowboy boots, fringed jacket. She was stunning. A surreptitious sideways glance revealed his DCI suitably stunned.

Collier had no intention of jeopardising his career by asking *Why have you come out of your office to stand in the corridor and watch a golden woman walk away?*

Hunter said, 'That's Willoughby's niece.'

Collier's gaze returned with new interest. 'She's been to see you?'

'Ye—es,' Hunter murmured, retiring for a fraction into a private place where the young Bette Davis might or might not feature. 'She thinks we're victimising him. Come on, I'll tell you about it.'

They went into the office. After listening to Hunter's account of Liz's visit, Collier said, 'The majority view. He wouldn't hurt a fly.'

'One dissenting voice.'

'The anonymous phone call.'

'Mmm. But I'll tell you what. Miss Liz Farrell, thick in the bosom of the Willoughby family and adoring them—Miss Farrell knows something.'

'About Willoughby?'

'I'm sure of it.' Hunter brooded. 'But if she believed it was relevant to the investigation, she wouldn't hold it back. She's too responsible. She's too bloody impulsive. There's something, though.'

86

CHAPTER NINE

It was out of the question to return to Paula's, to be skewered on her curiosity. If she went anywhere else in Hambling, Paula, given time, would track her down. She was tiresomely knowledgeable about where Liz was to be found on a Saturday. If she had no success she pestered Liz's friends, who couldn't stand her and had been known to hide in shop doorways when they saw her in the street.

So Liz went home, the instinct of the animal to creep into its cave. She made coffee and went up to her workroom. In Paula's house the clutter was threatening; here it soothed, turning the mind gently to creative thoughts.

She was still aghast at the thought of the anonymous telephone call. Who could be so malicious—so cowardly? But if she didn't do something soon, Paula would be round; she would catch Liz off balance and, with infallible instinct, know she was hiding something. Liz knew that—nagged, stared at—she had no hope of keeping the phone call to herself. And once Paula knew—Helen would know. Hambling would know. Given time to reflect, get her defences into place, Liz would be able to cope; in the meanwhile, an edited version of her visit to Hambling police station was manageable only at one remove. She went next door into her bedroom and picked up the phone.

Paula, eager to the point of sharpness, snapped, 'I thought you were coming back here. I was starting lunch for us. Well, what have they found out?'

Things were looking up—she had escaped one of Paula's meals—tasteless, shapeless plates of—stuff. 'Well, the name of the woman—it's Beattie Booth.'

If there was such a thing as the sound of someone thinking furiously, Liz could hear it.

Eventually, Paula said, 'Never heard of her. Have you?'

'Of course not, and I'm sure Reggie hasn't, either.'

'Where was she from? Do they know? Not from round here, that's for sure.'

'Chatfield. One of those tower blocks.'

'Oh, well . . .' In the derogatory tone *How could we possibly know someone who lived in one of those places* . . . Liz heard an echo of her own voice, of Helen's. She felt ashamed. They might just as well have made an unspoken pact to agree that Beattie Booth had a right to existence, yes, but only in places suitable to her—and that did not mean Hambling.

'Did they say why they'd got on to him in the first place?'

When you're lying, keep it brief. 'Only what they said originally. They had reason to believe he was in the area and might have seen her. Or

88

seen someone.'

'What do you mean—"had reason"? What reason?'

'Oh, God, Paula, I don't know.'

'And who's "someone"?'

'I can't exactly recall what they meant by that.'

'Well . . . You haven't got much, have you?'

'I don't think there is anything else.'

Paula made a rude, disbelieving noise. 'Did they assure you they won't bother him again?'

—No, of course not. How dare she hang around the police station, demanding assurances, when she'd almost put her foot in it disastrously. 'They're satisfied with his alibi.' *Were they?* Had anyone mentioned it?

'How did they treat you?'

She thought of a man built like a gun-slinger, with a watchful, determined face; eyes with the light of a winter sea; grey in his dark hair, an air of immovable calm.

Oh, God, fate throws Burt Lancaster at me and I make a complete ass of myself . . . I emptied my handbag on his . . . I called him a . . . She curled herself into a ball and moaned softly.

'*Liz,*' Paula yelled.

'What? Sorry, I—er just knocked something over.'

'You haven't answered my question. What was their attitude?'

'Um . . . polite. Helpful.'

Repetition of rude noise. 'And told you sweet f.a. What's their next move?'

'Good God, Paula, I'm not in their confidence. And why on earth should they tell me anything? It's nothing to do with us any more.

'Well, maybe that's what they said—it doesn't have to be true. I wouldn't trust the swine as far as I could throw them. So, what are you going to tell Helen?'

'Er—what I've just told you.'

'Not much help, is it? You might as well not have gone.'

Liz could no longer remember why she had; a flood of irritation was causing a log-jam inside her head. 'Paula, we're not going to get any further with this and I have a lot of things to do—'

Paula was inclined to persist, but only so far as Liz's patience stretched. Gauging its exact limit, she rang off.

Liz gave herself time to calm down; there was no point in phoning Helen with nerves shredded by Paula. She could only hope Paula didn't phone in the meanwhile, it was much better Helen receive her sensible version instead of something alarmist Paula had decided to make up.

She had a cup of tea, thought about things, phoned Helen. 'I went to see Paula this morning.'

'How good of you, darling. Do tell.'

'Well, she was upset on Reggie's behalf, that's what it was, really. That the police were making enquiries—'

'What enquiries?'

'Oh, just general things—backing up his alibi. But what Paula was getting so aerated about, she thought that, as his family, you—we—ought to know about the enquiries. Oh, well, the long and short of it is, I went to the police station.'

'The police . . . I don't understand.'

'I don't think I do now. It must have seemed like a good idea at the time. Perhaps I wanted to give myself up.'

'Liz,' Helen said with gentle reproof.

'I'm sorry. Two doses of Paula this morning —one at her house and one on the phone— and I can't seem to make much sense of anything.'

'Tell me about it.'

They talked for a while, Liz feeling herself soothed, explaining what had happened, reassuring Helen—who in turn reassured her—'It'll all blow over, don't worry about it. I can't think of anything more noble than taking Paula *and* the police on in the same morning. Do you feel like doing something else noble this evening?'

'Of course, what is it?'

Helen had forgotten (an indication of her distraction over Reggie, she was scrupulous about social engagements) that some time before she had invited two neighbours, the Dalrymple sisters, for whist—'and as Reggie's still away . . .'

'I'd love to,' Liz was hopeless at bridge but she could manage whist. And the plump little Dalrymples were adorable, very mischievous for two old spinster ladies. 'And it'll keep Paula away, to know we're there with you—she thinks whist evenings are too unbearably middle class.'

'You are naughty. Come early and we'll have supper together.'

*   *   *

The Dalrymples arrived under umbrellas and, after a delightful evening, left under them. They had been gone no more than five minutes when the front doorbell rang. 'They must have left something behind.' Liz cast around in the hall for a scarf, a handbag, while Helen switched the porch light back on and opened the door.

She screamed. Once, abruptly.

Liz flung herself at the front door, expecting to see somebody—somebody menacing standing there. At first, nothing, then, her gaze drawn down and to the side. Her heart thumped in her chest; without knowing what she was doing she had pushed Helen behind her. But Helen had already seen . . .

The sprawling figure. Rain slanting through

92

the carved columns of the porch, rain streaming off red plastic raincoat and white boots. 'Oh, my God. Helen, it's all right—I mean, it's not real—It's a sort of dummy.'

Helen's voice, faint and shaking, 'It's disgusting.'

'Yes, yes, it is . . . But it can't hurt you. And whoever put it there must be . . .' Liz stepped into the porch, past the shiny, bloated thing. She peered down the drive, although there was little point. Whoever had dumped this had been away like lightning and, on a night like this, with the shelter of the bushes and the shrouding rain, there would be no hope of following and finding them. She wasn't sure she wanted to. Besides, she couldn't leave Helen.

She went back into the hall, where Helen stood at the open door, she seemed unable to move. Liz put her arms round her, felt the fragile body quaking. 'God knows why anyone should do this, it's cruel and disgusting, but I'm here with you—'

'It's her, isn't it? It's meant to be that woman. Get it away from here, please.'

'Yes, yes.' She went to the threshold, indicating what she would do. 'We certainly can't leave it there, it's just too . . . At least it's no weight to carry. I'll take it through here to—

'Not in the house!' Helen cried.

'Only *through*. Listen, dear, please. I'm

going to take it straight through and out the back. You—don't look, go in to the sitting room or—' Without waiting for further argument, Liz crossed the porch, grasped the slippery, cold thing and went at top speed; hall, corridor, kitchen, back door. Out into the night, but under cover, in again to the old wash-house. There was a light, she put it on, stood getting her breath back, looking at the thing she had carried.

Apart from its effect of shock and disgust, the simulacrum conveyed with savage insult a judgement—or opinion—of the character, the conduct, the totality of the dead woman. The plastered-looking, painted-on hair, the round eyes, the vacant face, the open O of the mouth grossly connecting her with the furtiveness and isolation of substitute sex.

Liz, nowhere near as calm as she wished Helen to believe, felt shaken, angry and very uneasy. It could not be possible that what it was and why it had appeared were any way relevant to the woman's death—but someone was sick enough, and vicious enough, to bring it right to Helen's door and Liz wondered whether it would be wise to call the police. She switched off the light, locked the wash-house and went back into the house.

Helen was still standing in the hall, white-faced. Liz steered her into the sitting room, sat her down. There, incongruously, everything was as it had been from their gentle evening's entertainment: the satiny spread of light; the harmony of velvet, mahogany, gilded wood. She made for the oak sideboard, on whose splendidly gleaming surface reposed a collection of brilliant-cut Victorian glass: bowl and basket shapes deeply incised with the most extravagant ornamentation. She knew Helen particularly favoured it; she knew it was valuable; she considered it insanely awful and was always terrified of breaking bits of it—especially now, with hasty hands, reaching for the decanter, pouring two brandies. 'Come on, Helen, drink this, it'll help. I certainly need it.' She had said it before, but she needed to say it again. 'That thing can't hurt you.'

'Have you locked it in?'

'Yes.' As if it could get up and walk about in the night. Poor, poor Helen. 'It's terrible you should be persecuted like this—by someone very sick, very malicious. Don't you think it would be a good idea if we told the police?'

'Liz—no. Absolutely not. I forbid it.'

'All right, all right,' soothingly.

'This is *nothing* to do with anyone else, we must keep it to ourselves. I want your word, Liz, you will never speak of this to anyone. We must not let them know—this person who gets some kind of perverted pleasure out of doing this—that we have been in any way affected by it. We must get rid of it—it contaminates everything merely by being here.' She spoke fast and urgently. Liz thought—she hasn't pulled herself together yet, she doesn't know what she's saying. Thank God I was here.

'We must get rid of it, Liz. But where, where? There's nowhere to burn it—' her voice, caught on something like a sob, rushed on, 'It won't fit in the dustbin—unless we—we chopped bits off it—besides, we *couldn't* put it there—when the men come and open the bin—they'll see it and—that would be frightful. If we *wrapped* it—but then, when they got to the tip, the wrapping could come off, and everyone would see—and know we'd tried to hide . . . Can we somehow—dismantle it, Liz? Oh, could you? I couldn't *touch* it. But then—what . . . where?'

Her suggestions for disposal continued wildly and for a time unstoppably. Liz saw this was necessary: Helen must talk her way out of her shock, out of her obsession that this awful thing might be traced back to her—it would do no good asking who on earth would go to that kind of trouble and why should they?

At last, when Helen showed positive signs of calming down, Liz said, 'All I need to do is deflate it.'

'Deflate? How can you? Isn't it a model of some sort—a lay-figure?'

The term was horribly appropriate. 'No. I'm afraid it's something obscene. It's an inflatable woman.'

Amazement had a bracing effect on Helen—if only temporarily. 'Liz, don't be absurd. Whatever could it be for? Who would want something like that?'

'A man.'

'Why?'

'To use as a substitute for a real woman,' Liz said sensibly. 'We're somewhere very sordid with this, Helen. The person who could use such a thing as a means to terrorise you has to be pretty sick. I don't want to frighten you any more than you are, but I shall never stop worrying, knowing how vulnerable you are when I'm not here. That's why I'm telling you the truth about this. Helen, you must get Reggie to come back home. You shouldn't be here alone, you need his company and support.'

Every particle of Helen's fastidious nature must have been revolted by Liz's explanation; and yet in spite of her evident disgust there was, in an extraordinary way, something like a world-weary acceptance. Helen—who had no knowledge of the world—insensibly, wearily communicated—*oh, what next?* She had, Liz realised in that moment, unsuspected strengths. There was also, in the reminder of Reggie, the reminder of her responsibility to him, a lifelong habit nothing would dislodge. 'Liz, you'll never tell him, will you? I know you're sophisticated about these things, and he might be, too, but I would find it all too hideously embarrassing.'

'No, I won't tell him.' Liz didn't know about

97

Reggie and sophistication, she suspected that one look at the revolting object would frighten him speechless.

Helen went on. 'This was directed at him— through me. Sheer vindictiveness. That is why we mustn't show we have given in to it in any way.'

'Yes, I understand. But I mean it, Helen, he must come back and keep you company. Now, I'm going to make us a cup of tea and we'll work out how to dispose of that damn thing in the morning.'

They sat and talked, Helen more herself yet still brittle with nerves. Eventually, they decided that Liz, after deflating the lay-figure (the neutral term Helen insisted on) would cut it into little pieces, make up separate bags of the pieces, seal them with sticky tape, take them to the tip and distribute them amongst various skips.

At last in bed, Liz found it difficult to sleep. Out of her jumble of thoughts one surfaced that kept her awake for some time. Suppose the intruder had not used the front gate and drive for fear of being observed? Although there would have been few people about on such an evening, no one could carry anything more conspicuous. Suppose he—she—had used the path behind the houses—*knowing* the shrubs concealed a gate in the fence—and made their way through the garden. It would have been easy enough to creep round the side of the house, unbolt the wrought-iron gate . . .

She had no idea why the thought should occur to her, or why it should disturb her so much, but she couldn't shake it off and knew that in the morning she would have to go and check the back gate. The last thing she wanted was to alarm Helen by putting the thought into her head; and she could not think of a single, convincing reason why she should walk the length of the garden without explaining herself. Before she fell into an exhausted sleep she had worked out what she must do.

*　　　*　　　*

They were both up early. Helen looked as if she had been awake all night. It was a glowering day, dark as an old engraving, with squalls of the everlasting rain. Liz took herself off to the wash-house with far too many plastic bags, sticky tape, Helen's craft shears and a Stanley knife. Disposing of the lay-figure took a great deal of time and made her hands ache. But at last the job was finished. She stowed the bags in the boot of her car, acutely aware that every move she made was watched by Helen from inside the house.

They breakfasted, and when Liz was ready to leave—wearing the wellingtons she kept at Woodside and an anorak from her car—Helen said, 'I can't tell you what it means to me to have you help me through this, and be so brave and calm.'

Liz, feeling furtive and jittery, said gently, 'There's nothing to be afraid of, I'm sure. Listen, what we were talking about yesterday, about the police checking up on Reggie's background and everything. I've been thinking . . . they might contact you. If they do it won't be because I've told them about this, you can trust me.'

'But, Liz, why should they?'

'Well, they seem to need to ask about him and you know more about him than anyone. This is such a peculiar business; we have no way of knowing what people are thinking, saying . . .'

'I know. I can only hope that this vicious person has been satisfied by this act, and will do nothing else. And I do think the way we must look at it is that if their asking questions helps to settle this awful business, then we must co-operate as much as we can.'

Liz left, arranging to be in contact later. Once out of the gates, on to Woodside, she drove no more than two houses, slipped into a parking space under the trees, locked her car and went at a fast walk, with a sense of *déjà-vu*, along the path. It was impossible for Helen to see her from the house, but she felt conspicuous, lurking by the fence, studying the state of the shrubs, the gate itself—firmly locked. It was hopeless, she couldn't tell if the shrubs were more damaged than when she had thrashed through them on Friday; it didn't look as if the gate had been tampered with—although how was she equipped to judge?

She turned to go. Gasped aloud to find a figure almost upon her in the gloomy tree-tunnel. It was only a moment—the sense of menace in a deserted place—she felt limp with relief, recognising him.

'Made you jump, didn't I?' A gleeful chuckle.

'Mr Truelove, it's you.'

'Who else?'

Who indeed, in that place and at that hour of the day. Morning and evening, at unvarying times, he followed an unvarying route, no matter what the weather, brisk in his lurching stride. If he had worn his (up to now) unvarying clothes she would have recognised him at once. But in place of his shabby military mac and old tweed ghillie hat, he wore an entire outfit of smart, enveloping waterproofs.

His reedy laugh rang out, the heartless self-congratulation of the old. 'You should have seen your face. Didn't recognise me, eh? My daughter bought me these, aren't I splendid?'

Liz admired them, wanting to brain the old bugger. He made people scream with his cantankerousness. His daughter, mortified by his looking like a tramp but not wanting to discourage him from leaving the house twice a day, must have found it worth the fight to get him out of his old clothes.

As he was not remotely interested in anyone but himself, he didn't ask Liz what she was doing hanging about the end of Helen's garden. But he was unpredictable, so just in case, Liz said a cheerful, 'Bye now,' and was off. If she kept their encounter brief there was a good chance he would forget all about it and not start asking Helen awkward questions next time he met her.

CHAPTER TEN

In the old merchant area of Chatfield, broad pavements, stately squares, grand buildings, spoke of past wealth and confidence. At the close of the working day the business community surged homeward, leaving the city to the whisper of rain on shining streets, the ghosts of prosperous gentlemen driving home in their carriages.

The pub—the Brown Jug—having its interior grotesquely interfered with in the sixties, had been returned to an approximation of its origins with engraved glass, polished wood and pretend gas lighting. In an atmosphere so peaceable they might have been the only customers (there were, after all, very few), WPC Annette Jones and DS James Collier sat for some time with little inclination to say anything. After a while, Annette roused herself. 'Right. We've been everywhere. Well, everywhere this niece—this spinster schoolmistress—said.'

'Ah, yes,' Collier, thinking of the spinster schoolmistress, gazed innocently into space.

'The Manhattan. Merlin's. Bloody Barker's. Oh, Christ, everywhere. This Reggie is so vacuous he scarcely exists as an entity, never mind picking up someone like Beattie.' She sipped her drink, put her glass down carefully. 'This is the local brew, isn't it? We'd better take it easy, it's pretty strong.'

'Just one. We need something to eat. Shall we try that Thai restaurant? Unless you've got anything else doing tonight.'

'No, I haven't. That's a good idea.' There was no one waiting for her to go home, she was disinclined to cook for herself. In the intervals of affairs she claimed to be hopelessly in love with Hunter. Collier said she was only trying to make herself interesting. *Interesting . . . He never looks at me with a spark of interest, never mind decent galloping lust, the way a man should look at a woman. You know.'*—'I take it that's a rhetorical question.'

Like Annette, Collier was currently unattached; when he did have a relationship it was with a man. Annette found nothing remarkable in this except his ability to withstand verbal attacks of homophobia ranging from the crass to the savage. Looking like a school prefect, blonde and scrubbed clean, just about regulation height—if that had still applied—no one expected him to fight dirty. He had to, to survive. He loved being a policeman; where it came to defending his private life he was very, very tough.

(When Hunter first asked Annette if she could team up with Collier—could they work together?—she was enthusiastic. 'Oh, James is great. Not that I fancy him.' Hunter observed it was just as well. 'Yes, guv. I know.' 'Good, then there aren't going to be any problems.' None, she assured him, and there never had been.)

She looked round the pub. 'It's nice here, isn't it? Restful. James, why does Hunter always call pubs the Frog and Nightgown?'

'Only the ones he likes drinking in, I believe.'

She felt too peaceful to give this any serious thought, so they sat in communicative and undemanding silence until Collier said, 'He was doing it again today. Having a conversation with himself.'

'And you sort of fall into his mind, like falling into—a snowdrift. I have to dig like bloody hell sometimes to find out where I am, don't you?'

'It doesn't always do to bother. Not if it's private.'

Deeply interested in the private recesses of Hunter's mind, Annette asked, 'Was it?'

'Yes. The young Bette Davis. Her early

films.'

'Now you're doing it,' Annette said, then grew dreamy. She adored old black and white films. 'Her dresses. The way she *wore* them. The way she walked.'

'Yes, that was what he was on about.'

Annette examined this in the context of a working day, unavailingly. 'What, for God's sake?'

'Miss Farrell. Willoughby's niece. That's how she walks.'

Annette narrowed her eyes. 'Don't tell me.'

'Do you mean that?'

'No.'

'Tall. Slim. Classic beauty.'

And *you* said *he* said she's "very nice". What a cretinous understatement.'

'He also said she knows something.'

'I wish we bloody did.'

In from the whispering rain, the evening quiet, Constable George Withers appeared, bulky and smiling. They greeted him with pleasure. Collier went to the bar to get him a drink. Annette said, 'George, what can you be doing *out without your wife?*'

'No place for Enid when it comes to a wild night with a pal.'

'Don't be silly. You can't.'

'Why not?'

'Because . . .' He sat before her, square and solid in his civvies. 'People like you don't. You're everyone's uncle—cosy and full of

105

common sense.'

'I've always wanted to be sexy and dangerous.'

'Who is?' Collier delivered George's half pint. 'You'd better watch that stuff, George.'

'Weaned on it. And what are you two about?'

'Just collapsing at the end of an unproductive day.'

Collier said, 'Come on, Annette, I know we haven't turned up anything but there is the eye-witness. You up to date on that, George?

'Only that there is one. No details.'

Annette explained. 'A young woman, lives in Hambling. Thursday, Friday and Saturday she works as a night nurse at Chatfield General. She uses the old Hambling road because it's closer to where she lives than going through town to the by-pass. One Thursday evening, four weeks ago—she remembers because she was late and had to phone up and tell them when she'd be in. At the by-pass end of the road she saw a woman answering to Beattie's description getting into a white Mondeo.'

'Did she notice the driver?'

'No. She was so intrigued seeing someone like Beattie in a country lane in the middle of nowhere she never even looked at the driver, couldn't say if it was a man or a woman.'

'And it was just that one night?'

'Yes—because she was later than her usual time.'

'Right. What happened about the buses? She must have left a trail there.'

'True, but it hasn't led anywhere new. Still the bus shelter by the old Hambling road,' Annette said. Several passengers, she explained, had noticed Beattie, some chatted with her—just a few words—nothing that gave any indication who she was meeting, where she was going. But—the weather being so bad that last Thursday evening, there were few people travelling, no one was much inclined to speak, so no one could say if there was anything unusual in her manner. 'We've had nothing from the road check, though, and nothing of value in response to the press release.'

Collier said, 'Your turn now, George. Come clean, what are you up to?'

George had a way of looking at Collier: measuring, not unkind. He would accept Hunter's recommendation of any man, but he still needed a margin in which to make his own judgement. And if this nice lass thought so much of him, he must be pretty straight. So to speak.

'Your boss and me are having a night out, going round our old haunts.'

Annette said in a small voice, 'Can I come?'

Collier said, 'Don't take any notice of her, she gets weak-minded when she's tired. Ah, of course . . . You and Mr Hunter know this city inside out. You both grew up here, didn't you?'

'Man and beast.'

'So it's not just a night off, is it? I mean, some of this was Beattie's patch, too, wasn't it? George—did you know her? All those years ago?' Annette asked this with all the insultingly bright-eyed tactlessness of the young.

'No. I've tried to think back. There were hundreds of us kids. She might only have lived a few streets away, but still . . . there were invisible frontiers. You had to make sure you knew what they were if you wanted to survive, you know—'

No, they didn't know—sitting there eager and polished, with their Young Conservative background and university education. They were the product of what he had made sure his kids had—an upbringing in a sheltered suburb of well-kept gardens and parks. What could they know of survival on the streets?

'You mean, you're going to see if anyone can tell you anything about her, even something inconsequential?'

'It's all inconsequential,' Hunter said. No one had noticed him come in. He took off his trench coat; rain spangled his dark hair. As he sat down a waiter—previously indistinguishable from the décor—appeared at the table.

Collier said, 'Not for us, thanks. If Annette drinks when she's hungry she falls down.'

Annette kicked him under the table, said to Hunter, 'Inconsequential?'

'Mmm. Everyone's going to tell us something, and everyone wise after the event. It's the only subject round here. Poor old Beattie had to pop her clogs to get the attention she's getting now.'

Annette said, 'But, George, you've covered this ground, haven't you? *Ad nauseam.*'

'This is different,' George said. 'We're having a bit of a night out. We'll look in here, have a drink there, a chat, a bit of reminiscence—we're good at that. Egg and chips at a caff, mug of tea at the all-night with the toms and taxi drivers.'

'Return of the natives,' Collier murmured.

'You've got it, lad.' George said. Because he and Hunter, for all their well-tailored look, had that mysterious ability—the partial eclipse of self—that enabled them to graft themselves on to their surroundings: the familiarity with which they sat, the ease with which they talked; the confidence of their walk, the salt of their everyman humour. Their progress through the evening might be marked with furtive slinkings away, panic-stricken departures, nudges and nods—*watch them buggers, they're the Bill.* Still, they had their place in that world, they would talk and be talked to. They would listen.

Hunter took an experimental sip of his drink and sat looking at it in silent respect before saying, 'I've just come from Beattie's flat. Just taking a look round.'

He had no need to describe it, they all knew what it would be like: variations came in the range of possessions and degrees of cleanliness. Beattie's possessions were meagre, cheap, worn, pathetically clean. But here and there, gaudy proofs of affluence amongst all that was scrupulously brushed, scrubbed, mended . . . New matching duvet and bedroom curtains. New rug before the gas fire. New clothes in the wardrobe. If credibility could be stretched far enough to consider that Beattie had savings, any evidence of them would be in her still undiscovered handbag. (Another handbag, battered enough for everyday use, yielded nothing.) There was no cash hidden away in the flat. She was on Social Security, with nothing to spare. He had no doubt who was giving her money. Voluntarily? Or not?

He was being regarded expectantly. At any moment someone would ask him what he had found that forensic had missed. He felt apologetic. 'I didn't get anything out of the flat, but I did find a neighbour who had something. Well . . . Old girl one floor up from Beattie's. Knew Beattie by sight but not more than the occasional word. Except a few weeks ago—the old girl's husband was very ill—Beattie knocked on their door and said to let her know if she could fetch any shopping. That's about the longest conversation they'd had. Early September, the old boy took a turn for the worse, his wife was often up half the night, making tea, looking out of the window for something to do.'

Annette leaned forward. 'She saw them? She saw Beattie with him?'

'She saw Beattie getting out of a car. A white car. There's something in front of Causeway laughingly called the Concourse. Most of the lights are broken. There's so much shadow it'd be impossible to see inside any car.'

Collier said, 'Someone else who couldn't tell if it was a man or a woman driving.'

'That's it. But it *was* a Thursday night. The old boy was taken into hospital next day, that's how she remembers.'

George said, 'Well, there's always been the problem of how she got home. He drove her. Obvious. And at a time when there was hardly a soul about to see him.'

Collier said, 'And at the Hambling end presumably no one to ask why he was going backwards and forwards at all hours of the night. So . . . he lives alone?'

George said, 'This Willoughby doesn't, does he? Isn't his set-up with his sister?'

Annette said, 'She's not deaf, is she? I'm not being frivolous—but if she couldn't hear him going out, coming back late, it'd make her corroboration of any times useless, wouldn't it?'

Hunter said, 'I think we'll go and take a look at Miss Willoughby tomorrow, you and I,

Annette.'

'Right, guv. Did you get anything else from the neighbours?'

'I might have done, buggered if I know it means anything. Just gossiping here and there, one of them lives opposite the local laundrette, knows Beattie by sight. Apparently in the few weeks before her death, Beattie started going regularly into the laundrette, not carrying any washing. I went to see the owner. What happened was that every Thursday or Friday, Beattie went in there to use the phone. Being on private premises it's unvandalised. It's also private in the sense of being in a little lobby to one side of the laundrette. She couldn't overhear what Beattie was saying and Beattie never volunteered anything.'

They thought this over for a while. Annette said, 'It's significant in that it was an unusual activity for her, coinciding with the time she'd been seeing this man.'

'On a Thursday,' Collier said. 'Confirming their evening date. On a Friday—what?'

'It might have nothing to do with the investigation. But it'll give you an excuse to feed information into that insatiable instrument of yours.'

Collier agreed, and in a short while he and Annette went thoughtfully off in search of supper. Sitting companionably with George, Hunter picked up his glass, swallowed deep. 'This the special?'

'That's right.'

'Well, I'll tell you what, George. It'll take the wrinkles out of any bugger's scrotum.'

* * *

Late. George, completely sober, drove Hunter, not completely drunk, home to his flat on the outskirts of Chatfield—an exclusive development so featureless that in certain lights it looked like a cardboard cut-out. There Hunter lived, minimally, expecting nothing in the way of aesthetic satisfaction from his domestic arrangements; he ate out, he worked. At least the flat provided privacy, adequate for one-night stands although too stark for anything of a more regular nature. Affairs occasionally involving candlelight, recklessness and clean underwear were conducted in expensive hotels. Hunter took his lifestyle for granted; George considered it grievous. Glaring at the development from the car, he said, 'Bloody barracks. I don't know. You had it all. Wife, daughter, nice house, nice garden.'

'George, I was dying of boredom. I had those things because I thought it was the right thing to do. It didn't make any of us happy.'

'No. I know. But that's not to write the whole thing off. With the right woman, someone to provide a stable home life—'

'Bugger that. It's fun I'm looking for.'

George sighed, reverted to the evening's

113

business. 'What about Katie?'

Katie's Kaff. Katie herself, known to them both from their hot and undiscriminating youth, had got through two husbands without conspicuous grief. At present she was on holiday abroad doing the most raucous things she could think of, but her business hummed away at its usual rate because she had stamped her personality so firmly on it staff and customers kept looking over their shoulders for her.

Hunter said, 'She's a Mrs Wellbed in the making.'

'She always fancied you.'

'*Mrs Wellbed*?'

'No, you silly sod. Katie. So did that little punk waitress. I thought she was going to get inside your shirt.'

Waitress was a courtesy title on George's part. Katie's Kaff had skivvies who cleaned, cooked, washed-up, took your order and slapped down on your table a huge plate of delicious, cholesterol-stuffed food.

'I don't fancy fifteen-year-olds with nose rings,' Hunter said. Katie's staff would never speak out of turn—but they could hint. No harm in that. If anyone later checked on Katie, she could always know nothing about anything or (depending on who was asking, and why, and if it suited her) she could be a source of information.

George said, 'D'you think that kid was

having you on? Hoping you'd go back?'

'No. Katie'd have her magenta hair out by the roots. No, she wouldn't dare hint Katie knew something, had heard something, if it wasn't true. But . . . It could just be one of the lurid rumours that are going around.'

'We've heard enough of those this evening. D'you want me to follow it up?'

'No, George, I will. It's worth a call when Katie gets back.'

CHAPTER ELEVEN

Hunter and Annette stood in the porch of 18 Woodside. Annette rested her hand on a carved wooden column. 'Isn't it beautiful? Victorian? Edwardian?'

She spoke softly. The morning spread its hush about them: blurred shapes, the fall of a leaf. Sunlight behind mist softened the boldness of scarlet and yellow and russet. Hunter tried to think if he had ever been in a lyrical garden before.

The door was opened by a neat, grey-haired woman, crisp in a pretty floral overall.

'Miss Willoughby?' Hunter enquired.

She didn't say *certainly not* but she might just as well have done. 'If you'll wait a moment, I'll get her for you.' She went briskly away with a face full of pity for people who

115

couldn't tell the difference between the cleaner and the lady of the house.

Hunter murmured, 'Oops,' then he and Annette had nothing to do except stand looking through the open door into the hall.

Gleaming parquet; rugs in subdued tones of gold and green and blue. A cast-iron umbrella stand of Gothic design that would have looked mad anywhere else but here became a charming curio; a matched pair of mahogany hall seats, acanthus carved; a console table of inlaid rosewood.

Helen Willoughby appeared, elegantly dressed, graceful, a look of polite interest animating her fine-boned face. She must have been very beautiful once, Hunter thought; anyone can see her niece in her. He proffered his warrant card, began, 'I'm Detective Chief Inspector Hunter from Chatfield police station—' She took an involuntary step backward, her face rigid. He said quickly, 'Everything's perfectly all right, Miss Willoughby. We'd just like a few words with you. Forgive me for startling you.'

She recovered rapidly, nodding to Annette when Hunter introduced her. 'This has been a stressful time for us, and as my brother is away, I thought . . .' She did not appear to find it necessary to finish the sentence. 'Please come in.'

She led them to the sitting room. Long windows, a grand piano, gilt-framed mirrors reflecting softly luminous colours: cream, ivory, egg-shell blue. So much comfort and good taste Hunter felt as a reproach: you had to be invited, arrive in your best clothes, preferably by chauffeur-driven car . . . Playing the stolid copper, he moved with assurance about the room; no one would guess he was terrified of breaking something. 'He's still away, then? Your brother?'

'Yes. He should have come back this week but has rather a bad cold. We thought it best for him to stay in Cheltenham just for the present. I shall probably go and collect him this weekend.'

She was perfectly composed. Reserved, distant, but regarding them in turn with ladylike interest. If she wished them in hell, her carefully schooled expression would never betray it.

'You'll be aware by now, I suppose, that we've released the name of the woman whose body was found in the Chat. Miss Beattie Booth. Does it mean anything to you?'

'My niece told me she'd been to see you. You asked her that question, didn't you? My reply is exactly the same as hers . . .'

Annette had chosen to sit on a chaise-longue upholstered in ecru silk damask in an instantly dismissed moment of imagining herself reclining in a lace peignoir. She found herself looking glumly at the graduation photograph of a radiant young woman

117

who could only be the niece. Unobtrusively changing position, she examined several silver-framed photographs: always the young woman, an older man, Miss Willoughby.

In gathering information about Reggie, Annette had inevitably learned something of the family—the mother, who had died young; the dictatorial father; Paula and her two daughters. But they had no place here; here, where she reigned, Helen made her wishes plain: *these are my family, these are the people I love.*

'. . . whilst I would agree my brother is happy-go-lucky, he's truthful and an honourable man. I'm sure Liz told you so.'

Hunter, assessing the woman before him, gave some thought to the anonymous telephone call. In spite of his promise to Liz, if he thought there was anything to be gained, he would tell her about it. It would distress Miss Willoughby, yes. But . . . jolt her from her composure? No, he doubted that. Her defences were very securely in place. There was nothing to be learned by those means.

Sensing that Hunter needed to ponder something, Annette indicated a photograph, said to Helen, 'This is delightful. Is it your garden?' The four figures could have been left stranded from an Edwardian tea party: the two women sitting in falls of chiffon, sweeping hats, parasols daintily poised. The men standing, blazers, straw boaters—Reggie sporting a monocle. Not only was the group enchantingly composed, it differed from the other photographs in that a new figure had appeared: a man in his sixties perhaps, burly, close cropped hair and beard, extremely attractive. They seemed timeless, always caught in sunshine, willows around them—'it could be the real thing. But it's you, isn't it, Miss Willoughby.'

'Yes. And my niece, Liz . . . Reggie . . . and a friend of ours, Wilfred Heatherington. Liz helps with the costumes for Hambling Amateur Dramatic Society—well, when she can find the time. She's so gifted. They were doing *Charlie's Aunt* and we thought it would be fun to dress up in those lovely clothes.'

Hunter glanced at it. Grown-ups playing like children. It was very beautiful. Returned to business. 'Do you know of anyone who has a grudge against your brother?'

'No.' She was surprised. 'Why do you ask?'

'I understand there's been gossip about him.'

'The gossip, Inspector, has been occasioned by your actions,' Helen said, an edge to the dove-like voice.

'Has it?' he said interestedly, as if this had not occurred to him.

She was an intelligent woman. For an instant they measured each other, will against will. Her upright posture, firmly clasped hands, spoke of a lifetime of restraint; the open look

119

she turned on him said: it's a waste of time trying to provoke me. I know everything about self-control.

'During these last few weeks, have you noticed anything strange in your brother's behaviour?'

'Most certainly not.'

'No. Ah, I phrased that clumsily. I apologise. For instance, the night that concerns us—the night he went over to Midham—was this a normal sort of social pattern for him of a Thursday?'

'Well . . . there was no special evening for him to go to Robert's. Thursdays, weekends, any time really.'

'Yes, I see. And that evening, you were at home when he left the house?

'We more or less left together.' She was plainly not a gossipy woman, she would talk easily only to people with whom she was close, but she was patient, polite, taking trouble with the way she answered him. 'You see, it happened to be one of the evenings when I visit an old friend. She's more or less bed-ridden; a group of us have a rota, taking it in turns to sit with her, talk, read to her, settle her for the night. I stayed quite late, sometimes it's very difficult for Martha to get to sleep, day and night aren't always readily distinguishable to her. I came home earlier than Reggie, I did hear him come in, I think it would have been near midnight.'

'I see. Have you been away during the last few weeks?'

'Not since June, when we had our holiday together in Tuscany. Won't you sit down? Let me get Mrs Riley to make us some coffee.'

'No, thank you. I don't think we need take up any more of your time.

Annette said to herself—yes, please. I want to sit in this lovely room and have coffee from a silver pot and biscuits on a tiny china plate. I want to look out at the garden and listen to you telling me in your caressing voice how well the clematis have done this year, and how difficult it is to keep the eucalyptus pruned—

'No, thank you. Good morning, Miss Willoughby,' she said in her brisk, no nonsense way.

* * *

They had been shown out. The door was shut. Helen could be at any window, unseen, watching them.

Annette slipped into Hunter's BMW. He was slower, going round to the driver's door. As he opened it, a very dirty Metro turned into the drive, parked in front of the first garage. The young woman who got out gave Hunter a hard stare, let herself in in a proprietorial way through a wrought-iron gate at the side of the house, and disappeared. They looked after her. Her dirty car, shapeless coat, granny boots, could not have been more out of place. 'I'd say the cleaning woman only she's already there,' Annette murmured.

They fastened their seat belts. Hunter said, 'Well, we have ascertained that Miss Willoughby's hearing is perfect. No—you could have been right. Deafness plus a house that size—an army could tramp in and out and she'd never know.'

'I thought—from what I'd heard about her—she'd be an old dragon. You know, autocratic, cold, ordering everyone about like servants. But she's not. That . . . gentle grace . . .'

'Her charm's easy to fall for—why not, when it comes so naturally. Also a woman of considerable self-discipline.'

'Yes, that came across, too. But that's her type, isn't it? And she had to develop some means of survival, stand up for herself, protect her little brother. Their mother died young and by all accounts their father was a perfect old bastard.'

'Did he ill-treat them?'

'Not physically, as I understand it. Every other way. Drove them closer together.'

'There's something the niece said about them.'

'Would that be the spinster schoolmarm niece?' Annette asked dryly.

'Yes, that one. She said they live in their own world, where everything's polite and beautifully ordered. I understand now what

122

she means. There's not much room for harsh reality there.' Hunter started the car, turned out of the drive.

Annette glanced back. 'Beattie's posh house? With the garden big enough for a swimming pool? Even from the road you can see that, can't you? And it must apply to all the houses along here. But . . . look at it. What in God's name has any of *that* to do with Beattie?'

'Stranger things have happened.'

'You mean—Reggie might like a bit of rough?'

'Could be.' . . . I hope his niece does. I'll make her an offer.

Annette gave him a sideways look. You old dog. Right, you needed to question Miss Willoughby. You think the niece knows something. Right. But that's not *just* what this is about. You're hoping to stampede the beautiful niece into coming to see you again. You old dog.

*   *   *

Liz made her second visit to Hambling police station with a certain diffidence. At the front desk, in place of the short constable she had almost lifted off his feet (perhaps I've just come to say I'm sorry to everyone for behaving so badly) was a strapping young woman Liz would not have taken on at any price.

123

'Detective Chief Inspector Hunter: I'm not sure. I'll just ring through for you. People are always in and out, it's not easy to keep track. Who shall I say it is?'

Liz gave her name, waited, and after a few moments found herself sitting in an interview room facing two pleasant young people.

'I'm afraid Mr Hunter had to go over to Headquarters. Is there any way we can help? I'm Detective Sergeant Collier and this is Detective Constable Jones.'

Nothing in their ease, their smiling efficiency, indicated their breakneck reaction to her request to see Hunter—

(Annette: 'Who? *Who?* Don't let her go. Put her in an interview room. *Don't* tell her the guv's not here. James—I *said* she'd come in, didn't I? *James*, where the bloody hell are you?'

Collier—they are striding full speed down a corridor. 'If Hunter couldn't get out of her whatever it is, I don't see how we can. *No, of course* we're not going to pass up the chance, you silly besom—')

Liz, answering their smiles across the table in the dingy room, recalled Hunter's 'my team are professionals.' He couldn't have meant these—just two well-dressed people, as ordinary as any of her friends. She said to Annette, 'You went to see Helen—my aunt—last week, with Mr Hunter, didn't you?'

'Yes.'

'Was she all right?'

'Perfectly, as far as I could tell. Why do you ask?'

'Well, I haven't seen her since last Sunday. She left for Cheltenham yesterday. I spoke to her on the phone during the week . . .' To make sure she had recovered from the awful incident on Saturday evening, that there had been no repetition of it, or anything like it. During their conversation Helen assured Liz that the Detective Chief Inspector had been perfectly civil and the woman constable seemed a very nice type of girl. 'They just wanted to make sure for themselves I knew nothing about this woman.'

Reasonable enough, but Liz couldn't shake off an unspecified uneasiness. Was there a new, brittle strain to Helen's voice? She felt so out of touch.

'You didn't say anything about the anonymous phone call?'

'No, I think Mr Hunter assured you he wouldn't.'

'Yes. It's just that I worry about her particularly as Reggie's away.'

Collier asked, 'You've been in touch with him?'

'Oh, yes—' Liz spoke with the kind of enthusiasm intended to convey they were in constant communication. The barest truth was that of the several times she had phoned, Reggie had only once been available—scarcely that because he was just about to go out. She had written—an affectionate, teasing letter— not expecting a reply. Reggie was hopeless when it came to anything more than 'All my love' on a greetings card.

She said, wistfully, 'It's just that I'm always used to them being here, weekends, spending time with them. You're sure Helen was all right?'

It could not have been more evident to Annette that Liz was badly in need of reassurance. 'Miss Farrell, your aunt struck me as a very capable woman. She was as helpful as she could be.'

Liz looked shocked. 'But, of course, she would consider it rude *not* to be helpful. It's Paula who specialises in obstructiveness.'

'Paula?' Annette repeated. Her enquiries had accounted for Paula, although she was not aware she was the young woman who had arrived at Woodside just as she and Hunter were leaving.

'Helen's younger sister. She makes huge fusses about everything and upsets Helen. Me, too, to be honest, sometimes. She's an absolute pain in the backside. We never tell her anything.'

Collier said quietly, 'And what is there to tell?'

'What?' Liz's expression was fleetingly anxious. 'Oh, I mean silly things, family things. Nothing that really matters. Relatives can be absolutely . . . Heavens, is that the time? I really must go—' With smooth, unstoppable movements she was up, half out of the room.

'Miss Farrell—'

'So sorry. Appointment. Simply must dash—'

She had gone.

'James, you *silly bugger.* You scared her off.'

'I know. All right. It was too soon.'

'It was too heavy.'

'She wouldn't have reacted like that if she hadn't got something to hide.'

'We've blown our chance of finding out what that is, haven't we? James, you really are a silly bugger.'

CHAPTER TWELVE

The day was bitter with wind and grey with sleet. It was, fortunately, invisible from the steamed-up interior of Katie's Kaff. Katie, comfortably built, well-preserved and well-bejewelled, sported an unsuitable suntan that made the faces around her even more pallid than usual. She seldom smiled (a smile was something given away, violating her businesswoman's instincts) but she made exceptions for certain people. Hunter, for one.

'Hallo, Sheldon. Long time. Still married?'

'Yes,' Hunter lied serenely.

'Pity. I'd have you if you wasn't.' She placed a thick white mug before him, full of her ferocious tea: mahogany coloured, steaming. 'Fancy anything? It's on the house, seeing as it's you.'

She nodded to the menu board, an invitation to chronic ill-health. Fried bacon and egg balm cakes; jumbo sausages; steak and kidney in a suet crust; meat and potato pie; the best chips anyone ever tasted—with everything. And puddings: spotted dick, syrup sponge, jam roly-poly. 'No, thanks, Katie,' Hunter said, inwardly sighing. How many customers had fallen dead here of indigestion? Blissfully.

'Come into the office.'

The office was a cubby hole, fanatically scrubbed clean. Through a two-way mirror Katie could see into every corner of the café.

'You're looking well, Katie. I called while you were away. You'll have heard.'

'Will I now? Fancy . . .'

Compliments, banter, the necessary preliminaries. He was patient, savouring his tea. Eventually, Katie told him.

'Not seen hide nor hair of her for a couple of years—more. Course, she'd been shifted to Causeway or wherever on that rehousing. Even so, this hadn't been her stamping ground. Well, I'd heard her mother had died— poor old cow. But Beattie—you have to watch her with fellers, she was any bugger's as'd have

128

her.'

Hunter interpreted. Beattie had attempted to poach one of Katie's men. It could have happened years ago; grudges were long and hard around here. 'Fallen out with her, then, had you?' he asked blandly.

'Huh, she didn't bother me. I could sort her any time. Different story with my Vic—smarming round him—and him that good-hearted he was a fool to hisself.'

That was not what she'd said about him when he was alive. Vic. The second husband. (God, that *was* years ago.) Shaft anything on two legs. Perhaps she'd caught them at it. No wonder Beattie had stayed well away; Katie must have given her hell.

'So I was sat in here that night—about beginning of September—and I looks across to that corner and there she is, large as life and twice as ugly. I thought—should I clear her out? But she wasn't doing nothing and I wouldn't give her the satisfaction. Quite honestly, she wasn't worth shit. So I just kept me eye on them.'

'Them?'

'Woman she were with.'

'What was she like?'

'Just, like, ordinary. Nowt special.'

'Young? Old? Tall? Short?'

'Well, p'raps forty-ish, hard to tell. She'd not stick out in no crowd.'

'Had you ever seen her before?'

'No. I clocked her when she come up to the counter to order. I'd say she weren't from round here. We get all sorts passing through; but you get a feeling for locals. Anyroad, she bought a good tea for the two of them. Steak and kidney, chips, pudding. She paid. Beattie never gave her no money after, not as I saw and I kept a good watch on pair of 'em. Course—she's been on assistance for years so she's never had owt.' She used the outdated term—assistance—insultingly. All that Beattie's circumstances meant to her was a chance to exercise her contempt.

'Did they seem friendly?'

'Talking all the time, heads together. Thick as thieves, I'd say. Vera served them. I did tell her to hang around clearing tables, like, see if she could hear what they was rabbiting on about. But it were a waste of bloody time asking.' She indicated Vera, a fat, slow young woman of such bovine aspect it was obvious that if she had managed to overhear anything, she would have forgotten it by the time she got back to the counter.

'Then they went in phone booth—' She pointed to a glassed-in cubicle in the corner of the café; it had looped-back curtains and a kind of frill of plastic flowers. It was a 'facility' and as such Katie was proud of it. 'People come in and use it a lot. Well, it's private, and confidential, and not wrecked like all them outside. They both went in—well, they

130

couldn't *get* in—Beattie's half out while this woman dials, hands phone to Beattie. Didn't say nothing herself as I could see. After that, they left. Nobody left no tip.'

He turned this over in his mind. 'Is that all, Katie?'

'Well . . . Nothing to do with me, but about a couple days after, week mebbe, I was down in Kitchener Square market talking to Doris. You remember her, don't you? Has the pot stall. Right. She says, "You'll never guess who I saw the other night in the Railway. Beattie Booth. Not set eyes on her for years." Course, this was never her side of town even when she was living in Owen Street . . .'

Echo of long ago; the fiercely territorial children: *what you doing in our street*?

'Well, I said, buggered if I know why the old slag's started haunting us—and I told her about her being in the caff.'

'Did Doris say who she was with?'

'Yeah. Feller. Didn't know him and I weren't interested, so we left it at that.'

Hunter finished his tea. 'Katie, why didn't you tell us about this before?'

'No bugger asked me. Oh, George Withers come round, but I were away or summat. It were only when I got back and heard what had happened and there'd been all this asking about her. Anyroad, I've told you now. Does it matter? Does it mean owt?'

'I've no idea,' Hunter said.

Hunter and Doris sat together under the lifted hatchback of Doris's Volvo where they were out of the rain and Doris could keep an eye on her stall. There was little business about on such a miserable day; the wind had grown sharper, sending greasy chip papers flapping across the cobbles of Kitchener Square. It was a squalid area, the buildings run-down fifties development, flimsy and falling to bits; nobody cared about them now.

'Dead odd, that. I mean, neither of us setting eyes on her for years—then we both seen her the same week.' Doris poured from a flask. 'Sure you won't have a drop? Keep the cold out.'

'No, thanks.' God knew what the concoction was. 'Had a mug of tea at Katie's.'

'Well, that'll set you up. Not that you need any help.' She eyed him, nostalgic lust. 'Allus was a big bugger. Did you know Beattie?'

'I don't think so, Doris. If I did, I can't remember.'

'I don't think as you'd forget, she'd of made a dead set at you. She were a devil when she were younger. She calmed down—well, we all has to, don't we? Middle-aged spread, bunions, false teeth. Mind you, she were still a looker—that's what I noticed first, not having seen her so many years. And *that's* what made

Katie pig sick. Allus hated the sight of her. Then to find she'd worn better nor any of us. Trouble was—Beattie were a loser. Fellers taking her for a ride—and she let them. Just like her mother. But, you know what they say—where there's life there's hope.' Unaware of any irony, Doris continued. 'So when I see her with this feller I thought—leave her to it.'

'You didn't speak to her?'

'No. You know how quiet it is in the Railway early on . . .'

. . . it was always quiet round that part of Chatfield. Once there had been a teeming sense of busy lives lived to some purpose, but with the closing of the railway, the businesses, shops and workshops that had been necessary to it and supported by it, stood abandoned, boarded up. There was no vandalism, no graffiti, not much litter. No one went there much any more; the buildings, monuments to civic pride, had taken on a certain grand, grimy melancholy. The Railway, a splendid example of brewer's gothic, would have lost its reason for existence but for humankind's enduring thirst.

'There was hardly no one in. I were round by side of the bar with Vi—my sister-in-law, we allus has a few on a Thursday—I had me back to the door and Vi pulls a face and says summat about Lady Muck, so I looks round and there she was—Beattie Booth as I live and breathe. Turned herself out special, ever such

133

a nice blue jacket and dead high heels. Summat told me not to let on, I says to Vi—"I knows her, but don't say owt." So we shift round a bit so we can both clock her. She just kind of stands there, waiting, between bar and door. And then—in he come. Walks up to her, says summat, shakes hands—honest—takes her to a table in corner—I'm not kidding—see she's comfy, like, then comes to the bar. We could just hear him, real posh—proper, not put on. Then he takes the drinks back to their table. Vi—she's never known Beattie—says, 'Aren't you going to let on?' I said no, I'd rather watch because, honest, it were as good as telly. There *she* was, Lady Muck all over, and him, well . . . He were a real gentleman, written all over him, not one of your piss-artists. And I thought—where the fucking hell did Beattie find him?'

'Can you describe him to me, Doris?'

'Fortyish. Average height. Fairish. Beautiful dresser—blazer, white shirt, tie. Nowt gaudy, just—well, proper.'

'How long did they stay?'

'Only the one drink. It weren't his kind of place. I doubt Beattie had set foot there nigh on five years but she were at home all right. Him, no. He looked around, like—dignified, not sneering or owt but . . . not his kind of place. So they gets up and goes out and he holds door open for her—I'm not bloody kidding—and out she sails.'

134

Hunter, hopelessly, began, 'Doris, you know we've been asking—'

'Oh, all right. But this were months ago.'

'Seven weeks.'

'Well . . . And you *know* why. You know my old man. He'd kill me if he thought I'd told you the time. Don't think you can come back to me on this—I'll not admit I've said nothing.'

'No,' he said, far away. Mentally unreeling Doris's account he had only just caught up with its significance. He had got an eye-witness to Beattie's first meeting with Reggie Willoughby.

CHAPTER THIRTEEN

Miss Devere sent for Liz during afternoon break. With no premonition of disaster, Liz, making her way to the big, book-lined study-cum-sitting room, amused herself inside her head with the girls' favourite chant. *Miss Devere is severe.* True. Also dignified, unfailingly kind and just. Years before, she had lived and taught in Hambling, a particular friend of Helen's. Two of a kind.

'Liz, come and sit here, beside me.'

Liz looked cautiously at the big leather sofa. It was less a piece of furniture, more an emotional anchorage: for confidences, comfort, for uncounted little girls sobbing out their homesickness, their sins, their fears.

Miss Devere's firm, cool hand rested on hers. 'Liz, I have some bad news for you.'

Liz thought, clamorously, *not Helen* . . . was dumb, waiting.

'It's Reggie. I'm so sorry to have to tell you, my dear. He's taken his own life.'

Her immediate reaction: don't be silly, he wouldn't know how to, he's too inefficient. But the only word she could articulate was, 'No . . .'

'This is a terrible shock for you. I know how fond you were of one another.'

'How do you know?' Accusingly, as if Miss Devere had just make it up.

'Paula telephoned.'

'Oh, *Paula* . . .'

'Yes, yes.' Understanding. Miss Devere knew all about Paula. 'But Helen is much too distressed to speak to anyone, and you had to be told straight away.'

'Go on, please.' It was, painfully, becoming real.

'You know he returned from Cheltenham on Monday. It was this morning. Helen was out, one of her committees, then luncheon. When she got home the garage doors were shut—his garage—she could hear an engine running. It was fortuitous that she'd almost immediately been followed down the drive by Paula. So they were both there. Helen didn't have to find him alone.'

'Only this morning? It's Thursday.' Why was she saying such stupid things?

'Liz, listen. Go home this afternoon, then stay on after the weekend if you think it necessary. Helen will need you, and no one can help her the way you can. You're going to have to be very brave, take a lot on your shoulders. I know you can.' Thus the certainties of Miss Devere's high-principled life.

I can't. I can't do anything. I can't even cry.

'Now,' Miss Devere said in her rallying voice. 'You are going to be all right to drive, aren't you? Sure? Yes. I shall telephone you this evening at Helen's to see how you are. All right?'

'Thank you, Miss Devere.' For being so beautifully organised. Please continue to hold me together. I shall fall apart.

*   *   *

No, she didn't fall apart. Helen needed her. There were movements to be performed, stately as a saraband; mundane matters where she displayed her organisational ability, her authority. But Helen's face was like a mask from a Greek tragedy; her eyes empty. She stayed in her room, scarcely speaking, clutching Liz's hand tightly. Sometimes, without warning, she would fall asleep, escaping into oblivion. Liz understood that. If only she could. Behind her grief and bewilderment—guilt. *If I hadn't insisted he return home he would still be alive.* Would he?

Does Helen blame me?

There was Reggie's suicide note. Liz had not seen it, but Helen had—and, of course, Paula, who found it with her (something, for once, to thank God for, that Paula was there). The police had taken it; in their jargon they had 'seized' it. Not that that mattered, Helen could quote it.

Dear Helen, Forgive me. I'm sorry about Beattie. What I'm doing will settle everything, you'll see.

'. . . his handwriting, Liz. Awful, sliding about. Usually so neat. But he had been drinking—well, there was a glass and the whisky bottle. And all those tranquillisers he had been taking . . .'

'Darling, darling.' They clung together, Liz unable to resist amazement at the conciseness of the message—when they both knew he could scarcely write a literate sentence. No, that wasn't fair. He rambled, he said everything twice. But . . . There it was, unequivocally (as Paula with her talent for uncomfortable truth pointed out) an apology, an acknowledgement. 'It says everything, Liz, doesn't it? That he knew her, that he . . . And he asks Helen's forgiveness.' Paula was subdued, uncharacteristically sensible, and tactful enough to speak to Liz out of Helen's presence. 'You didn't see him when he came back from Cheltenham. I did—only very briefly, he seemed to want to hide himself away.

138

Understandable now. Of course, Helen said it had done him so much good being away—because that was what she needed to believe. But, Liz, he was a wreck. Completely zonked on tranquillisers, and he was drinking. We thought it was just his general weakness, but, of course, it was guilt.'

Liz had to agree; the inner self that denied it all was quenched. She asked Paula, 'What happened?'

The day after he returned home, Robert invited Reggie over to Midham. He was the one person Reggie seemed to want to spend time with. As the amount of tranquillisers he was taking made it unsafe for him to drive, Helen chauffeured him there. He spent a quiet day with stout-hearted Robert, doing little jobs, doing nothing. He arranged to go again on the Thursday because Helen would be out all morning and through lunch time and he couldn't bear to be alone in the house. Paula agreed to drive him to Midham. 'It was just before I was about to set out, when he phoned. He said he'd changed his mind, he was very tired, he was going to stay in bed. He said he'd phoned Robert and told him not to expect him. I asked if I could do anything—go round and make his lunch, but he said no. So I left it at that. Liz, if you'd seen him, how exhausted he looked, you'd understand why I took that on trust. I know I shouldn't have—' Paula, assertive, always right about everything, faltered, acknowledging error. 'It wasn't till early afternoon. Something, I don't know, a niggle, a premonition. I phoned Robert—he hadn't heard from Reggie at all, but knowing the unpredictable state he was in, just left him to do as he pleased. That started alarm bells ringing. I drove round to Woodside straight away. Just as I turned the bend at the end of the road—there was Helen's car, turning into the drive.'

Liz listened, helpless against an unfair thought: if only she'd had her bloody premonition an hour earlier.

'I pulled up in front of the house directly behind her. As soon as we'd both switched off and got out of our cars—there it was—the sound of an engine running. From inside his garage—the doors closed—'

'I'm so sorry you had to find him. It must have been dreadful. At least, Helen wasn't alone.'

'She just went into shock, completely numb. I was on auto-pilot, doing—well—trying to do what needed to be done . . .'

Liz then performed an action for which there was no precedent in her memory. She went over to where Paula was sitting, put her arm round her shoulders and held her for a moment. 'Thank you, Paula.'

*   *   *

The post mortem was performed the morning following Reggie's death and at the beginning of the next week the inquest was opened for evidence of identification, then adjourned.

Helen demonstrated the resilience of the human spirit by making a noticeable recovery; if she was not her usual self she was exercising enough control to function with something of her customary poise. Her many friends closed round her, tactful, discreet, efficient: armour plating against the outside world. They even had enough genteel ruthlessness to cope with Paula, who quickly grew fretful, demanding attention.

Liz, adrift in a cloud of uselessness, assessed the situation and took the opportunity to say to Helen, 'What would you think if I said I feel I ought to go back to school?'

'I'd say you are completely right, my dear. You have your work to do, and Barbara Devere has been more than generous allowing you time off to be with me.'

'That's it, you see. Strictly speaking, as I'm not an immediate relative, I'm not entitled to compassionate leave. I don't want her thinking I'm taking advantage.'

'Really, as if she would.'

'And—later, I can take leave officially, when I can be of use. I mean—the inquest. Then— Reggie's funeral—'

'Yes. I hope, darling, not to put too many burdens on you, but I will need you then.'

CHAPTER FOURTEEN

Hunter's interview with Chief Superintendent Garrett was brief and at times snarling.

'Christ almighty, Sheldon—we've got his confession in writing. What more do you want? I know all about your bulldog instincts, but you're just going to have to get your jaws out of this one.'

'He didn't say it in so many words, did he? He hasn't coughed pushing her off the bridge, has he?'

Glaring, the DCS said slowly, 'People can be understandably cryptic when they're about to top themselves. Now. Listen. At the start there was the anonymous phone call naming him. He goes into a nervous breakdown after being questioned. There was an eye-witness to his meeting with the murdered woman. He committed suicide leaving a note saying he was sorry about her. There are no suspicious circumstances surrounding his death.'

A small and telling silence. 'He had an unbreakable alibi.'

'There's no such thing.'

'There is if it's genuine.'

'Don't. Try. My. Patience.'

As it was already in shreds, Hunter considered he had nothing to lose. 'We wrap it up now—Beattie's killer's out there.

Laughing.'

The DCS leaned forward, white-knuckled. They were at the end of all the arguments; in the nature of things, he had to win. 'Have you had the *sniff* of another suspect? Have you? No. Now. I'm going to say this once and once only, so make sure it penetrates your thick skull. *As of now* this investigation is closed. Closed. Right? Right.'

*   *   *

Hunter spoke to his troops, formally, in the about-to-be-dismantled incident room. 'The DCS has ordered me to write this investigation off under Home Office rules.' Informally— 'You've all put a lot of work into this, and you may not agree with what's happening, but— technically speaking—the Old Man is right. I don't need to tell you anything about slashed budgets—we just can't afford to do anything except play it by the book. Sorry, chaps. End of story.'

Various reactions were displayed; some— not so evident—could be discerned only in a feeling of dissatisfaction, a subterranean unease. Annette and Collier had the look of children sent home from school on an unwanted half holiday. 'Guv—do you think Willoughby did it?'

Hunter was working on instinct, not evidence, but there was too much gap in rank

143

for him to be entirely frank. 'He did something. I'd lay good money on it. He's in there somewhere, sure enough. But then . . . so is someone else.'

*   *   *

The inquest was re-opened the following week. Evidence of Reggie's state of mind; the excess of alcohol and tranquillisers in his bloodstream; the suicide note indisputably in his own handwriting—all these pointed to an inevitable verdict: 'He took his own life while the balance of his mind was disturbed.'

Helen, dignified, subdued, gave evidence as she was required. Her friends spoke admiringly of her courage but Liz sensed a havoc of grief and bewilderment behind the public face. She was right. The inquest over, Helen collapsed.

During the ten days Liz had been back at school, Paula had grown weepy. At the inquest she had been called to the stand but, having nothing to add to Helen's statement about the finding of Reggie's body, she was dismissed. This filled her with resentment at the attention focussed on Helen. She took to following Liz about—red-nosed, clutching a damp, balled-up handkerchief and grizzling she was just as traumatised as Helen. Liz had to stop herself yelling, *For Christ's sake, this isn't a competition.* A useless restraint; Paula had decided it was.

Since Reggie's death, Liz had had to put her own feelings aside; she was not even sure what they were any more. All the funeral arrangements fell upon her—there were offers of help, willing friends and relatives—but still, she carried the burden of doing, being, what Helen would wish; it was only too plain that Helen would not be able to attend her brother's funeral.

*　　　*　　　*

A day of fragile mist and sunshine without warmth. Liz wore a fine black wool coat with a velvet collar, tiny waist and full skirt. She felt frozen and miserable.

From Woodside she travelled with Paula and Paula's two daughters in the first car as chief mourners. Paula wore a squashed hat of purple velvet, a black cloak and granny boots. For some reason she had dressed her two girls to look like Victorian orphans. At eleven and thirteen they had her thick build, large faces, wide mouths full of tombstone-sized teeth, dazzlingly white. Every so often they looked at each other and wordlessly, from no known cause, burst into rich, spluttering giggles. Liz could only assume these were a form of communication, in place of speech.

She said wearily, 'Girls, will you be quiet.'

They made goggle eyes of alarm. Hands

145

clapped over mouths, giggles escaped in small explosions.

'Paula, for God's sake tell them to behave.'

Paula, dull, red-eyed, said, 'My nerves are shattered, after what I've been through. I need to go away for a while. Rest. They should be with their father.'

'Well, they're not, are they? They're here and they're your responsibility. Why on earth did you let them come?'

'They have to learn to express grief in a social context.'

Muffled shrieks.

'Anyway,' Paula went on mulishly, 'you're the teacher, aren't you? Aren't you supposed to be able to keep order?'

'Not at Reggie's funeral,' Liz hissed.

Fortunately, the drive to the church was short and, their father immediately in evidence, the girls raced to him—pushing aside anyone unfortunate enough to be in the way—and began to jump up and down, flapping their arms and squealing *daddy, daddy, daddy*, like six-year-olds. He bent to speak to them and Liz noticed that almost at once they quietened. What did he use? Threats? Money? She sagged with relief to be rid of them but Paula—who should have been as heartily glad they had removed themselves—watched balefully for a while, then went to join them. The noise level began to rise.

146

Liz was more aware of representing Helen—and being a credit to her—than her own grief. She thought that, in the consoling ritual of the funeral service, she would absorb and be reconciled to the sad manner of Reggie's death. With so much to do and arrange and think about she was painfully conscious that she had not yet said goodbye to him.

The vicar, knowing him well from his occasional, good-humoured attendances at church and church functions with Helen, spoke sincerely of him; the choir sang heart-rendingly—but no rite of passage, no matter how dignified by tradition or sustained by feeling, could survive Paula's daughters.

With their father ordered by Paula to place himself elsewhere, they sat with Liz and Paula in the first pew. When the service was in its opening moments, and they had grown tired of twisting round and pointing at people and giggling, they listened, ominously silent. They dealt in surface emotions: this was mourning—they tried out their roles. Loud, competitive sobs, nostril punishing sniffs, collapse. Paula ignored them. Liz knew herself at screaming point. Thankfully, they disappeared at the end of the service, then reappeared at the grave, scuffling, shouting, '*I* want to throw dirt on him, me.'—'No, me first, I'm oldest—' They barged into Liz who said, low-voiced, 'Listen, you little rats—'

Beside her, someone said quietly, 'Liz.'

She turned to see the young woman police constable. 'Oh, it's—'

'Annette.' She gave a small smile, encouraging, wicked, then unceremoniously hustled the two girls to one side. 'Right. You've had enough attention for one day. Everyone's completely fed-up with you. Now. Your father. At once. He'll keep you quiet. One, two, one two—'

She did not exactly frog-march them away but they went at a speed that suggested she had, leaving Liz and several other people staring after her in admiration and relief.

Liz moved amongst the people who had gathered to say farewell to Reggie. Friends from the golf club and cricket club, neighbours, colleagues—Liz managed to speak to them while at the same time avoiding Reggie's boss who, with the most insincere look of sympathy she had ever seen on anyone's face, was in avid conversation with, of all people, Paula. Robert was there with his spry old father, talking to Wilfred, who semaphored encouragement to Liz.

There were tensions; strangers who had come to whisper and stare at everyone (this being the gruesome equivalent of a Hambling society wedding); people who were known to have enthusiastically spread rumours about Reggie. Perversely, Paula chose to visit her wrath not on these interlopers, but upon

148

Wilfred. 'What's he doing here? Fucking cheek.'

'Why shouldn't he be? He was very fond of Reggie, and he's Helen's friend.'

'*Friend*—oh, God, there you go again. So prurient, you school marms. He wanted to get his end off, that's what it was, and just buggered off when it suited him. And listen, I don't know what you were doing in the front pew. Strictly speaking it's for the closest relatives and you're too distant to be visible— I've never managed to work out the relationship between your mother and Helen. Apart from the fact that they hated the sight of one another. No . . . instead of you, it should have been Uncle William—' Sweet, vague Uncle William, taking one look at Paula's daughters, had fled to the back of the church and hidden himself amongst sympathisers.

Liz said, 'I don't know what the hell you're talking about. I know you're being damned offensive and I've had enough. Don't you dare bring those two girls back to Woodside.'

Paula looked thoughtful. 'In a sense, you know, they'll be a replacement for Reggie in Helen's life.'

Speechless, Liz stared at her.

'Well, he was Helen's child, really, wasn't he? She's always resented other people having children—it's understandable, never having the chance to develop her own parenting skills. Well, father . . . you know what he was like—

149

completely disempowered her, even deprived her of a normal sexual relationship—and everyone needs that for their mental health. No—her bonding's been confined to Reggie, she'll find it hard to accept his death totally—before she can accept a surrogate. She's got a lot of bitterness to dump. Not only this long-standing sense of missing out, but the betrayal—'

Annette appeared, got hold of Liz and took her away while Paula was still speaking. She said, 'I've had a word with their father, he's quite sensible. He agrees it'd be a disaster to take them to Woodside—although Paula seems set on it. He's going to drive them to Chatfield and let them destroy McDonald's.'

'Thank you. One day I'll do violence to that woman.'

'I'll help you.'

'I'm sorry I can't invite you back to the house, I feel it wouldn't be quite—um—This is embarrassing.'

'No, don't be. I don't expect anything of the sort. I came to pay my respects—and to see how you are. You look as if you've just about had it. You're standing in for Miss Willoughby, I believe. I'm sorry she's not well.'

'It's just all been too much for her. She managed wonderfully at first but . . .' Liz shook her head sadly.

'Now *you're* managing wonderfully. But for goodness sake, when you've got all this over and done with—you must get some rest.'

'I shall. I'm going to sneak away. I've arranged it. There'll be guests at Woodside till late but I don't need to keep playing hostess— a friend and a cousin will be staying overnight, and dear Uncle William—he won't be useful but he'll be a wonderfully soothing presence.

'Where are you going? Is it a secret?'

'Yes, my secret. My little house. To shut the door, and be by myself.'

'Are you sure that's a good idea?'

'Oh, God, it's a marvellous idea. I've had enough people for the present.'

'Yes, well . . .' Annette scribbled on a piece of paper. 'In case you feel like company, or a chat—any time. That's my private number.'

'I don't know what a nice girl like you is doing in the police force.'

'I'm bossy.' Annette's gaze was fixed beyond Liz, on Wilfred. 'I saw his photo at your aunt's, didn't I? What *is* it about older men?'

'Dunno. But it works, doesn't it? Would you like me to introduce you?'

'No, thanks. I'm going to sexually harass him. Well, what else can he expect—standing around asking for it.'

'Annette, if you stay here you'll make me laugh out loud and that's inappropriate at a funeral. Now, go and pick up Wilfred, he'll enjoy it.'

It was a long day. At Woodside there was not too heavy a spirit, and a great deal of affection for Reggie. When most of the guests had gone, only relatives left, Liz found herself standing in the hall, rather stupefied and empty-feeling. Wilfred appeared, took her hand; as if by the most sympathetic instinct, they both turned. Helen had at last emerged from her room. Hesitantly, bravely, she came down the stairs.

Liz and Wilfred held out their arms, enfolding her. If anyone came and saw, they went quietly away while the three stood in the house that Helen had filled with happiness for Reggie. They talked, inconsequential, silly, enchanting memories; they mourned . . . oh, if only . . . they wept. At last, Liz said goodbye to Reggie.

CHAPTER FIFTEEN

Liz sat numbly, her only emotion relief for her solitude. She did not feel she was deserting Helen, she had, for the moment, nothing left to give her. And there were good people, only too willing to care . . .

She thought of going up and comforting herself with beautifully useless jobs in her workroom, but she was too tired and continued to sit, in the shelter and peace of her house, her mind doing nothing at all. Late in the day an angry wind had come up, she could hear it, battering about in the darkness.

The doorbell rang. She thought she would not answer, but the lights were on—whoever was there would persist. She went reluctantly to the front door, switched on the porch light, looked through the spyhole, blinked. Opened the door.

'Hallo, Liz,' Hunter said.

The night was wild about him, the wind tossing moon-silvered shrubs. Eventually, Liz said, 'Um.'

'I know. Annette told me you needed to be alone. She also said you were exhausted, she was worried about you. I thought you wouldn't mind if I hung around very quietly for a while. I won't even speak if you don't want me to.'

She would never have believed this tough, impersonal man could speak and smile so kindly. Tears threatened. 'Oh, bugger.'

'Yes,' he said, struggling with a laugh.

'You're going to make me cry. Please come in.'

They sat in silence for a while. The fire was dying low. Hunter efficiently piled on logs, dusted his hands, looked at Liz—who was gazing in the flames. No golden aura now; her face was white and strained, her hair had lost its sheen. He wanted to fold her quietly, securely, in his arms. 'Liz, have you had anything to eat?'

'Oh, yes. Bits of things on and off all day. You know funerals. Moveable feasts. I know—

let's open a bottle of wine.'

They went into the kitchen. To him, her house was a jewel casket, glowing with soft colours, delicate, welcoming. Even the occasional untidiness seemed to be artistically arranged. In an automatic way, she set a tray with glasses, bowls of crisps and nuts, a plate of savoury biscuits. He opened the wine. 'Do not have anything in your houses that you do not know to be useful or believe to be beautiful.'

'William Morris. Have you just paid my house a compliment?'

'Several.'

'Thank you, Detective Chief Inspector—do I have to call you all that?'

'Sheldon.'

She received the name with interest. 'That's nice.'

He carried the tray for her into the sitting room and put it on a small table; she sat on the rug in front of the fire, long legs curled under her. The wine brought a little colour to her face. She said, 'That note was all wrong. I know. I know he wrote it, you proved that with all your tests. But the phrasing—that wasn't Reggie. You don't know—he waffled and wandered; he couldn't write a note to the milkman without taking an entire page. He'd never expressed himself so clearly—so briefly.'

He'd never been *in extremis* before. But Hunter couldn't say it.

'And there's something else. It seemed, at first, that saying "I'm sorry about Beattie" was an admission of guilt—but I've thought about it and I know what he really meant. He never knew Beattie, he never had anything to do with her, much less caused her harm—*that's* not what "I'm sorry" meant. No, he was apologising to Helen for the trouble and distress she'd been caused because—for no reason—he'd come under suspicion. I've talked to Helen about this—well, as far as it's possible to talk to her at present—and she agrees with me.'

She looked at Hunter decisively, with the air of something at last accomplished. He gauged her resilience. For all that fine-drawn look she was young and tough. It was better she know now; she could find out later, somehow, and think herself treated lightly.

'Liz, I'm sorry, you're wrong. I have to tell you this. On the day he died, I spoke to a woman who saw him with Beattie. Very probably, it was their first meeting.'

She was very still, upright, hands tightly clasped. It could have been Helen sitting there, if Helen ever sat on rugs before the fire. 'Go on.'

He told her about Doris, what she had told him of the evening in the Railway Hotel.

When he had finished, she thought for a while then said, not very convincingly, 'It might not have been Reggie.'

155

'I'm satisfied it was.'

'All right, all right. Yes, I was wrong. So he did meet her. Had—some kind of association with her—'

'Then why did he deny it? Not only to us—that's understandable—panic of the moment. But to his sister? If it was innocent?'

'Well, good God, innocent . . . You've *met* Helen, how could he admit he was having a bit of something—or not, as the case may be—with someone she would find so . . . unacceptable. I think he was ashamed, and ashamed he'd lied to Helen. That's why he got into that state, the mental strain was too much.'

'So he took his own life.'

'I don't think he did.'

Perhaps the strain *she* had been suffering all day had now proved too much; she was obviously tired out—perhaps a kind of wild despair was taking over . . .

'What are you saying?' he asked gently.

'I don't think he had the resolution or the competence. I'm convinced he didn't write that note unaided. Someone was with him, someone—helped him on his way.'

'That's completely inconsistent with the facts.' He looked at her steadily. 'You're talking about murder.' It was mad. Who had she got lined up as suspect?

'Someone murdered that woman, didn't they? And we know it wasn't Reggie. Someone made that anonymous phone call to you . . .'

Someone came out of the dark with that obscene lay-figure to torment Helen.

'. . . Someone went round to Woodside that morning, when he was alone and not capable of protecting himself. Amongst the neighbours—there'll be somebody who saw something, I know, I know. But you never made enquiries, did you? Can't you now?'

He sighed inwardly, faced with one of the illogicalities of extreme emotion: now that her uncle was dead, she wanted the police to prove him innocent. 'Look, I'm sorry about this, I don't think you understand. It's nothing to do with me personally—it's where the job's concerned. The matter's closed.'

'You mean, you're just going to leave it there?'

'I don't have any choice. As far as the bosses are concerned—your uncle was responsible for Beattie's death.'

She sat in silence for a while. Had he been too brutal? No. She looked at him with quiet certainty. 'You don't think Reggie did it, do you?'

It was the one question he didn't want her to ask, because beyond the simple answer his professionalism was threatened. He'd slipped up. It had taken this tragic outcome to force him to acknowledge that in the very beginning his diligence had failed; in concentrating on Reggie to the exclusion of anyone else he had

157

overlooked something crucial. It was there somewhere. He didn't know what or where but in everything he had learnt and seen and listened to—the moment had occurred. And slipped past him . . .

'I did think so—at first. But now . . . No.' As the investigation was closed he was jeopardising nothing by his admission. He thought she might get excited, accuse him, demand something be done, but she seemed satisfied, nodded and said, 'Well, no . . .' quietly to herself.

He saw that the day had suddenly taken its toll, all the emotion, all the control, draining away and leaving nothing but weariness. He had had an account of the funeral from Annette; her description of Paula's daughters set his mind reeling—anyone else but Annette and he wouldn't have believed it. 'We can talk about this another time, Liz, if you want. You're just too tired now. You ought to go to bed.'

'Yes, I think I'm beginning not to make sense . . .'

He put the guard in front of the fire. Carried the tray into the kitchen, saw the back door was locked, switched off the light.

She was still sitting on the rug. He reached down, lifted her, and for no more than a moment felt her slender warmth against him. He led her into the hallway. 'I'm going now. All right?'

'Yes. Thank you for keeping me company, it was kind of you.'

He kissed her forehead, opened the door, let himself out into the wind-thrashed night. *Thank you for keeping me company* . . . She had taken him at face value. As his sympathy was genuine he had no trouble with his conscience; he would never take advantage of her. It didn't seem to occur to her that he had the inclination to. That was because she was a nice girl. He couldn't see that getting in the way of anything.

* * *

Liz woke early, unrefreshed, her brain buzzing. If two resolutions were forming she recognised only their components and left them to arrange themselves while she showered and breakfasted. Her first duty was to Helen.

Instead of driving to Woodside, she rode her bicycle, which she loved. Pedalling briskly through a morning of dramatic gloom, of shrouded distances and skeletal trees, the air sharpened by the acid smell of decaying leaves, she had time to consider how she was to implement the first of her resolutions. She was so absorbed she found herself flying across Miller's Bridge before she even realised she had reached it.

This turned her mind in another direction and she cycled on more slowly, thinking over what Hunter had told her about Reggie's encounter with Beattie at the Railway. At some time she would have to tell Helen, but not immediately; that would be putting too great a strain on her sorrow. It would wait a while.

At Woodside there was still a hush in the atmosphere but the sense of a household under tension had eased, giving way to a distinct feeling that the comforting routine of everyday life was waiting to nudge itself back into place.

Mrs Riley had come in and was busying herself cleaning up after the previous day. Audrey, the cousin, and Catherine, the friend, gossiped cosily before the fire in the sitting room with a delighted Uncle William. Liz said to Mrs Riley, 'He remembers how ghastly it was here when he used to come and stay when old Mr Willougby was alive, he didn't have a home of his own, being at sea such a lot. He does so love it now. I'm afraid you might find him rather difficult to dislodge—don't be surprised if he's still pottering about in a few days' time.'

'He's a lovely gentleman, and he can talk to your aunt about Mr Reggie, she'll like that.'

'Stop all that busying, let's join the others for coffee in the sitting room.'

'No, I'll get on, I've the Dalrymples later. I must say, it was ever such a nice funeral—well, if such things are ever nice. Apart from, well, I prefer not to mention.' Like so many people, she preferred never to mention Paula's daughters. 'And people said such nice things about Mr Reggie. And it was all very elegant here yesterday, you arranged this beautifully, just as Miss Willoughby would've done herself if she'd been well enough. I hope she perks up soon.'

'Thank you, and thank you for all your help yesterday, I don't know what we'd have done without you.' Mrs Riley had been very fond of Reggie and stoutly refused to countenance any rumours about him.

Helen had been left to sleep, so Liz was in time to take her up her breakfast tray. She looked gaunt, fragile as a cobweb, but she was all ready, sitting up in bed in peignoir and pretty boudoir hairnet, her face made up. She knew the value of habit and discipline, she would put herself together slowly by such efforts.

Liz found this so brave she had to blink away tears, busy herself with the tray, then sit chatting for a while; arrangements for the day . . . a suggestion Mrs Riley be given a present for her help at the funeral. 'Yes, yes,' Helen agreed. 'You mustn't let me neglect such things. It's just—ordinariness—isn't it, that brings one back on an even keel eventually.'

'Yes.' So in Helen's beautiful room they talked of the most ordinary things .
. . . and beyond the echo of their voices—

the great, dark tract where some things would never be ordinary again.

Reggie's car still out there in the garage. No one had the faintest idea how to mention it, much less what to do with it.

CHAPTER SIXTEEN

She had no intention of telling Helen what she was about. When she had some results—whatever they might be—and when she could decide what to do with them . . . well, then would be the time to think again.

The houses on Woodside were set far apart, some a long way back from the road. Liz chose her target area. She knew most of Helen's neighbours by sight or by name . . .

I do hope you don't mind my calling (the advantages of being socially acceptable—she had always been accepted without question as Helen Willoughby's niece, it scarcely seemed to matter what disgrace had overtaken the family).—Do come in, my dear. May I say how sorry . . .

I know this might sound rather strange—but on the morning my uncle died—did you see anyone going into Woodside? No, not the postman, milkman . . . Just anyone.—Well, no, unless I happen to be out there with the dog . . . Driving Mother to . . . Taking the children

. . .

A blank at five houses; one left, final fling. The latest arrival on Woodside, Mrs Maltravers, wonderfully chaotic evidence of her family life all around her. 'Please, Miss Farrell, forgive all this mess. We haven't straightened ourselves out yet, and I've just got my husband off to work, the children off to school.'

'Don't apologise, I understand. Now, I know you're new here and—' calculatedly—'I do hope people are making you feel at home.'

'Your aunt, such a lovely lady . . . Invited us for drinks . . .'

'Yes, yes. I know this may sound strange, but my aunt and I are so concerned about my uncle's death. I've had some thoughts about it that she doesn't know, she has to take things very gently at present—so I'd appreciate it if you didn't say anything to her about this. I don't suppose that, on the day Reggie died, you can recall seeing anyone—a stranger—anywhere about.'

Mrs Maltravers, briefly, put her arm about Liz's shoulders—which no one else had done and almost reduced her to tears. 'I am so sorry, such a sweet man. Well, I wish I could help but—strangers—I'm not sure yet who is and who isn't.'

'Do you remember the morning? Did you see anyone at all—going into Woodside? Walking past?'

163

'I do remember that morning, yes, but it was just so ordinary. Arthur took the children off to school that day—I did the bits and pieces one needs to do, scraping porridge off the cat, that sort of thing. Then about ten I went up to one of the back bedrooms, putting up curtains. So I wasn't looking out of the front at all, I'm afraid. And on such a ghastly day who would be about? Except, of course, the old boy who walks down the back every day, nothing seems to keep him in.'

'That's Mr Truelove, he lives with his daughter in those new houses on the Nantwich side of Hambling. But he . . . Didn't you say you'd just got the children off to school—and tidied up—so it couldn't have been very early, could it? What time do you think?'

'Time. Ah, time. Is it important?'

'Well, I think it might be, rather. You see, old Mr Truelove never, never, varies. Mornings, 8.30.'

Mrs Maltravers gave a small yelp. 'I'm still on auto pilot then, not *doing curtains*. Let me think. While I was upstairs I listened to the end of the morning service; some of *Woman's Hour*—coffee time. Yep. About a quarter to eleven.'

'You're sure?'

Mrs Maltravers was a steady woman. She was sure.

'But you thought it was Mr Truelove?'

'Only because I've seen this old body

occasionally, striding out in all weathers. It's never occurred to me to look at the clock. I just assumed it was him—all bundled up in his rainwear—but if you say his time's 8.30, then . . . might he have altered it?'

'That's what I'd better find out.'

She pedalled off to Delamere Gardens, a good two miles. Mr Truelove's daughter, Martha, sat her down with coffee and biscuits. 'You need it, cycling all this way.'

'Thank you for coming to the funeral, I'm sorry I didn't have time to chat. It was good of you and your husband—'

'The least we could do, pay our respects. Reggie was one of the old school. I hope Miss Willoughby's feeling better, she's been through such a lot.'

'Yes, thanks, she's recovering, but it'll take time. Look, there's something I want to ask you . . .' Liz recited her story. 'Mrs Maltravers was the only person who saw anyone, and she thought it was your dad.'

'No, Liz, it couldn't have been. It was the last week in October, yes? Dad had already gone away by then to my brother's in Bridlington. Still there—God be praised—I wrote and told him about—about Reggie.'

'Well, the thing was, Mrs Maltravers said she saw him walking along the path behind the houses—you know how he does—only she said it was about quarter to eleven. And I thought, if he'd altered his time for any reason, and *he*

165

might have seen something, and if I could ask him . . .'

'Liz—catch him altering his routine by as much as a minute. No. And he'd gone away by then, so whoever it was . . . Mrs Maltravers is new, isn't she? It's understandable she'd make a mistake. One person in rainwear looks the same as any other, don't they?'

'Yes,' Liz thought, pedalling home. On a decent day there'd be some hope of identifying them, even across a distance, but in the rain . . . For the first time she thought of the drama and mystery of rain. How it weeps and whispers. How people dressed for it are almost in disguise, identity extinguished by turned-up collars, enshrouding macs, oilskins, caps, sou'westers, scarves . . . She sighed. It could have been anyone walking down the path behind the houses.

Back at home she put her second resolution into effect by telephoning Annette, who was delighted to hear from her. 'Liz, you sound much brighter.'

'Thanks. Now, I don't know what you're going to say to this. Listen quietly till I've finished.'

Annette was quiet even after Liz had finished, then, having thought, she said reasonably, 'What on earth do you think you're going to gain by this?'

'I don't know. Something. Nothing. Your boss said he was quite sure it was their first

meeting, from what that woman—Doris—told
him. A man can't talk to a woman the way
another woman can. If I talk to her—and her
sister-in-law—I can possibly find out
something that will help.'

'Help what?'

'I *have* to find out the truth.'

'You have to prove your uncle's innocence.'

'Yes.'

'The two might cancel each other out.'

'All right, I'll cross that bridge when—ouch,
that was an unfortunate phrase, wasn't it?
Annette, I know it's a lot to ask you to come
with me. But it has to be tonight. It's Thursday,
Mr Hunter said this Doris and her sister-in-law
are always in the Railway on a Thursday,
sitting at the side of the bar. We could find
them, we could—I won't *be* here next week,
Annette, I have to be back at school on
Monday—'

Annette had more objections, Liz more
persuasions. She was confident enough—
just—to go alone, but she'd be much better
with Annette, even a reluctant Annette.

'I do understand why it's important to you,
Liz, but you have no idea—it could be damned
unpleasant. You're not the type to fit in there;
if these women decide they don't like you—
and they don't have to have a reason—they
could be pretty nasty. Oh, well . . . I suppose if
you are set on it you'd better do it with a
professional minder. But listen . . . I'm running

the show.'

'Yes, constable,' Liz breathed.

Annette put the phone down. Collier, who had been hanging about deliberately after hearing Liz's name, came to sit on the edge of her desk. She told him. He said, 'I don't think the guv will like it.

'No, neither do I. Don't tell him, will you.' She did not need to ask. They looked at each other thoughtfully for a while. 'I like her, James.'

'Yes, she's nice.'

'I need to keep an eye on her.'

'That, too.'

'Besides, suppose I *did* find something I could take to Hunter . . .'

*   *   *

Liz was right. The Railway was so quiet they picked out the two women at once: sitting at a table to one side of the bar—a dumpy woman dressed in bright colours and a thin woman with a harsh face and orange hennaed hair . . .

Annette went straight to their table, smiled in an undifferentiated way. 'Doris and Vi?'

They looked at her warily. 'Who wants to know?'

'I'm Annette, she's Liz. We'd be ever so grateful for a chat with you ladies—we think you can help us, well, help her. It's about Beattie Booth.'

Liz was wondering frantically what had happened to Annette. The clear diction of her speech, slipping into the local accent, had become slovenly; her manner was pushy; she had even acquired a brassy smile. Careless and friendly, she had subtly aligned herself with the two women. Liz, not daring to open her mouth, felt like an alien species . . .

At Beattie's name, their interest sharpened visibly, but wariness prevailed. 'What's it to you?'

'Listen, we'll sit down and tell you all about it. What about a top-up before we start, eh? Come on, girls, no harm in us having a drink together, is there? What you having?' She took their order and was off to the bar. Liz, in a state of panic, shot after her. Their half-whispered conversation took place beneath the smirking scrutiny of the barman, who was gazing hotly at them.

'Annette, what am I going to do? I can't talk like you.'

'Why should you?'

'So they'll accept me.'

'They wouldn't accept you if you were gift-wrapped. For God's sake don't try, you'll sound like a send-up of Nora Batty.'

'Nora Batty is a send-up, isn't she? Here, let me pay for these—'

'No, I will—'

The barman leered. 'Not seen you girls here before. Looking for summat special, are you?

169

Anything I can do?'

'Yes. Fuck off,' Annette said.

Liz carried the tray with the drinks. Annette flopped down at the table. 'This is nice. Cheers, dears . . . Thing is, it was you saw Beattie meeting that chap in here, wasn't it?'

'How come you know?'

They had talked of nothing else for weeks, to anyone who would listen—and everyone did. But discussion was contained within tribal boundaries; Annette, as a stranger, was required to explain herself.

'I've got a friend knows someone at the nick—*no*, not a nark. And anyway, apart from that—you're famous. You know, nobody's ever got to the rights of it, and you're the only ones who ever saw them together. You do know that, don't you?'

'Yeah, well . . .' Heads inclined in synchronised, queenly nod, acknowledgement of their status. They lit cigarettes and disappeared behind a screen of smoke. Orange hair said, 'You mean him as done her in.'

Liz said quietly, 'He didn't. He didn't murder her—'

'Oh, no, not *much*—left a note saying as he did then topped hisself. That's what I heard. You know different, do you?'

'It's what people are saying, I know, but it isn't true. He was miles away from the place where she drowned—'

The dumpy one in bright clothes said, 'I'll

say this, Vi, we'd never have thought he'd harm a fly.'

Vi made a disgruntled noise; she was one always wise after the event.

Liz said, 'I know he wouldn't. I'm his niece.'

They reacted with a kind of indignation: how dare she come here, being who she was? Then curiosity, naked, fixed and—for the moment—speechless.

Annette said, 'You see, she'd just like you to talk to her about him. You know how it is when someone's passed on, you feel you've sort of . . . lost touch.' This largely true statement was delivered with a fraudulent sentimentality that had its effect in a change of expression—on Doris's face, at least; but both women continued to sit, not speaking, smoking and staring at Liz.

Liz said, 'There's so much we, his family, don't understand. He never said anything to us about Beattie—we didn't even know he *knew* her. Not until after his death, and then I learned that they met here. And you were the witnesses. Would you tell me about it?'

Doris said grudgingly, 'Told the big feller.'

'Oh, *well*, he's not likely to give nothing away,' Annette said with a great show of cynicism.

'You're dead right there,' Doris agreed. 'Know him, then?'

'You could put it like that.'

'Bit young for him, aren't you?'

171

'Am I?' Annette looked innocent.

Vi was spoiling to intervene. 'Didn't you say as he had a wife, Doris?'

'Wife?' Annette repeated, wide-eyed.

Side-tracked by their interest in Hunter, they had the air of settling down for an evening of sharp exchanges. Liz took a hand, speaking directly to Doris. 'What was she like—Beattie?'

'Well, I'd not seen her for years, but I can tell you, she'd worn bloody well.'

'Mind you . . .' Vi was not to be left out. 'I didn't reckon nothing to what she were wearing. A bit, well . . . plain. From what I heard tell she liked to flaunt it.'

'Yeah, well . . .' Doris pondered. 'She looked more the type as would suit him.'

Annette said, 'Do you mean you think she was dressing specially to appeal to him?'

'Well, we all has to, don't we? You know fellers—won't walk down road with you if they think you'll show 'em up.'

Liz wasn't sure why she found this interesting and—sensing a diversion into the preferences of males—decided to leave it till later and speak to Annette. 'I mean, Doris, what sort of a person was she?'

'Well . . . just like anyone. Just . . . ordinary. Never had owt, but that weren't her fault. And allus letting fellers string her along.'

'You mean, she had lots of boyfriends?' Liz asked.

172

Doris gave her a look of great forbearance. 'If that's what you want to call 'em.'

'Were they—do you think—from round here? Or people like my uncle?'

'Not fucking good enough for your sort from round here?' Vi asked aggressively.

'Come on, Vi, that's not what she meant,' Annette said placatingly.

'What did she fucking mean, then?'

Liz held on to her patience. 'You see, we don't even know when or where they met.'

'They bloody met here—or are you too stupid to catch on that's what we've been talking about? All the same your sort, bugger all on top.'

Stridently, Annette began, 'There's no call for that—'

'I don't know what you're getting so frigging aerated about, Vi. Do summat bloody useful for once and go and get some more in.' Doris produced a well-stuffed purse.

'Let me,' Liz said.

'No, you put that away,' Doris ordered. 'I know you mean well, but we're not short of a bob or two round here.'

Apologising, Liz felt Annette relax. She understood now why she had said this might not be such a good idea.

Temporarily relieved of Vi's truculent presence, the atmosphere lightened. Doris said earnestly, 'I understand what you're getting at, love. Well . . . I *think* I do.' Her face took on a

173

pained expression indicative of complex thought. 'They might have *met* here—but it were as if they—like as if they was expecting to.'

'Yes, that's it. That must mean they had some prior contact through . . . I don't know,' Liz said. 'After all, Beattie didn't just come and stand here on the off-chance. Yes?' Doris's expression caught her attention.

'Well, you saying she come and stood there. That's just what she did—but expecting, like. Standing in middle of room, looking at door. I mean, if she'd said, like, beforehand, on phone or summat—said, "I'm blonde and I'll be wearing a blue coat." Well—he couldn't miss her.'

Liz smiled at her. 'I knew you'd have something to tell me.'

Annette said quietly, 'Liz, it doesn't get us anywhere.'

Vi returned, plonked the drinks down, directed a poisonous look at Liz, then sat staring into the distance, ostentatiously ignoring everyone. Doris gave an eloquent tilt of her head, mouthed, 'Take no notice.'

'Doris—would Beattie have been the sort to go to a dating agency?'

'Well, I don't know about that. Them places cost money, don't they? and I can't think of no one as I know round here ever done such a thing. Would he have, your . . . uncle?' She hesitated over the word, looking away as if she had committed some social blunder.

Liz sighed. 'Reggie was potty enough to do anything just for a lark—if someone else suggested it. He never thought anything out for himself, but if someone put him up to it . . . but he'd have told me.

Annette asked, 'Would it be the sort of thing he'd tell your aunt?'

'God, no, she'd think it bad taste. He hated her to know if he'd done anything she disapproved of.'

'Did he—er—have women?' Doris enquired delicately.

'Quite a few girl friends, on and off, no one special.'

'He were well set up. I can't see he'd need to go to no dating agency.

'I can't either. But you know, Doris, I think you're right—what you said about Beattie describing herself beforehand—"I'm blonde and wearing a blue coat" and standing waiting there—'

Vi, dying of silence, said, 'And looking at door. Plain as owt, that was.

'Oh, come round, have you? Good of you to favour us with your attention,' Doris said mildly.

Vi chose not to hear. 'I mean, minute she walked in, she looked round, quick like, didn't take no notice of us. Well, she might of if she'd seen Doris on account of knowing her—but you had your back to the door, didn't you?

And then, she didn't go and sit down or owt, just stood there. You'd clocked her by then, hadn't you? and you was telling me about her.'

Doris nodded sadly. 'Fool to herself she was, with fellers.'

'Just like her mam, you said, Doris, didn't you? And exactly the same thing happened to her.'

Liz was aghast. 'You don't mean—you don't mean her mother was murdered.'

'Not *exact*, Vi, not exact. No, she weren't done in. Near enough, mind, left for dead.'

'That's what I mean,' Vi snapped. 'Beat up and left for dead by this fancy feller as no one'd ever seen. Well, that's what you've said often enough, Doris, told any bugger as'd stand still long enough to hear.'

'Yeah, well, you suddenly remembers these things. All this carry-on called to mind her mother and *her* mystery man. Supposed to be summat special he was, shitting diamonds or summat. Well, to hear Beattie tell it, though she were only a kid at the time, and allus a liar. Still, it were odd . . .'

Liz and Annette exchanged glances. 'Annette, did you know about this?'

'I've heard the occasional comment about her mother, but . . .' Annette shook her head.

'Tell us about it,' Liz said.

Doris sat in impressive silence, ordering her thoughts. Vi made a loud, exasperated noise. 'You know it by bloody heart, I don't see as

176

there's owt to think about.'

'The young lady doesn't want a lot of unrelevant details. It were like this. Beattie'd be about twelve. Just her and her mam. No bugger ever knew who her dad were, least of all her mam. Now, her mam was a lovely looker—'

'Bit of a hooer, too,' Vi interposed.

'So what? Plenty of those about; if you can get owt out of a feller, I say good luck. And she had to make the most of her looks while she'd still got 'em. She weren't *really* on the game,' Doris said to Liz, as if this would in some mysterious way reassure her. 'Bit of part time. Well, God knows there's enough of that allus gone on. And she kept her and Beattie clean, nicely turned-out, you know. She weren't no slag. Anyroad, she gets this special feller, has a bit of money to spend, and Beattie swanking her drawers off about how posh he is and he talks la-di-da and he's going to take them away to live in this big posh house. Buckingham friggin Palace to hear her. Not that she'd ever seen it. All talk, you know, all talk. And they got her out of the way sharpish when he called on her mam.'

Annette said, 'You mean he called during the day?'

'Well, there, you've said it. It were obvious. He takes an hour or so off from work for a bit of the other, then, end of the day, back home to his wife and family.'

Liz said, 'I thought—I thought you said—nobody ever saw him . . .'

'Well, they didn't hardly at all, love. He never took her mam out, for a drink, like, nothing. Never seen about with her. And nobody knew owt about him—because, it were bloody obvious she didn't. And he'd come—tall feller, dark overcoat, collar turned up, trilby hat pulled down—and he'd walk dead fast, like coming out of nowhere. Down back alley—*never* street—back alley, in through yard. Anyone standing about he'd go straight past, head down, never look no one in the face. Then it'd be getting dark by time he left—it were that time of year—and he'd be off like Phantom of the Opera.'

Annette said, 'What did Beattie call him—when she talked about him?'

'Now, that's asking. Apart from "me mam's new feller" you mean? That's how it started out; then summat like Arthur . . . Alfred . . . Arnold . . . It's that long ago. *Then* she says he's going to be her dad. Well, *that* took some swallowing, I can tell you. Nobody believed it, but I distinctly remember her saying it, only a couple of times, mind, not long before he put in his last appearance. Beattie were out playing and she'd managed to get herself invited round to tea somewhere, so it's quite a bit later than usual when she gets back home. Her mam's not in—that's what she must have thought, anyroad, cos she—I don't know, messes about, whatever. Then she finally goes upstairs, door to her mam's room's open—and there she is, lying on the floor, beaten senseless. So Beattie's off down road, knocking on doors, getting neighbours out, frantic, she was, frantic. Someone got an ambulance and they took her mam off to hospital. But as for him, well, he'd long gone, long gone. And you see, poor cow, she were never same after. She were weeks unconscious, and when she come round—brain damage. She couldn't remember nothing, what had happened, who she was.'

Liz said, 'But the police—surely they tried to find him.'

'Police? What's it to them? Another slag beaten up—happens all the time. And nobody could say who he were, you see, no name, no description, not where he were from—nothing. Beattie couldn't hardly describe him, not as made sense to find him, anyroad. She still had one or two relatives round here, then—auntie, cousin. And neighbours were really good to her. When her mam came out of hospital, she managed—' she smiled at Liz's involuntary surprise. 'Kids can, you know. Maybe not your sort, but round here—leave 'em to it, they get on with things.'

Annette asked, 'Was there never any sign of him again?'

'Not him, not a sausage. For all he knew she were dead. And reely, you know, she weren't fit for nothing. Needed looking after. Had her

179

good times, got a bit of a job, cleaning—but then she'd not turn up, or get things in a right mess—she couldn't help it, it weren't her fault. They'd sack her, she'd be living on assistance, as it were then, and bloody mean they were with it, I can tell you. Sometimes they'd cart her off to the funny farm, but they never kept her there long—she weren't mad, you know. Just, a bit daft, and Beattie were around to look after her.'

'Poor things,' Liz murmured.

'But then,' Vi said stridently, 'buggered if Beattie don't go and do same thing. Believes everything some feller tells her, finishes up in river.' Her triumphant look fastened on Liz. 'And him vanished into thin air—till he confesses and tops hisself.'

'You just hold your horses,' Doris said. 'Not the young lady's fault. She were fond of him and if she says he didn't do it—'

'What else she friggin going to say? What were he doing here, anyroad, in first place? And now her, turning up. Their sort bring nowt but trouble—'

'Now you just listen to me, Vi Twemlow,' Doris began.

Annette touched Liz's arm. 'Time we were going.'

CHAPTER SEVENTEEN

The air was cold. The melancholy surroundings had taken on a grimmer aspect— a personal message of past violence, spoiled lives. Annette said, 'We need supper.'

'Mmm,' Liz said absently.

'How do you fancy Thai food?'

'Super. Do you know—'

'I know you're building a fantasy. No—wait, wait. Talk while we eat.

'But—' Liz turned a troubled face to her. Her expression cleared suddenly. 'Annette, thank God you're *you* again.'

The food was excellent, the restaurant quiet. They sat in a warm corner, soothed by scarcely-heard music.

'You have to admit, Annette, that we have learned something. Tenuous, yes, but it does take us a little further forward.'

'Where?' Annette asked, looking at her with sympathy.

'Well, no one's suggested before that their meeting was arranged through a dating agency—some third party.'

'That's not a fact, that's supposition.'

'All right. But not entirely unsupported. Doris was very astute—what she said about Beattie dressing in a way that would appeal to whoever she was going to meet—you

181

remember? It seems that Beattie normally dressed in gaudy, well, common clothes. Reggie would have run a mile at the mere sight of her. But she made sure she looked presentable to him. Because someone told her to.'

Who?' Annette asked cautiously.

'The person who murdered her. Don't look like that. *Somebody* did and you *know* it wasn't Reggie. The person she was with that Thursday night and *that* wasn't him. The person who made the anonymous phone call. Now. The extraordinary coincidence of her repeating that episode in her mother's life—'

'Stop there, Liz. You know about human nature. There's nothing extraordinary about a life of deprivation where all the patterns repeat themselves because there's nothing anyone can do to stop them. Poverty, prostitution, violence . . . And the parallels aren't exact—there's a superficial similarity, that's all. And don't forget, we've only had Doris's version—and that, God knows, will be compounded of gossip, hindsight and local mythology.'

'I shouldn't have said coincidence, I got a bit carried away. This is the point I'm coming to. I agree, Doris's version is bound to have undergone all kinds of variations—but she did know Beattie and she did know her *at the time*. As a grown woman she's made assumptions about the relationship—but she was right what she said about the kids round here—self-sufficient, knowing, even as a child she probably had an instinctive grasp of the situation. And I wouldn't doubt the clarity of her recollection of how Beattie referred to this man—he evolved from being just another boyfriend to being her "Dad". Well, in the context of that relationship it's obvious what was happening, isn't it?'

'Is it?'

'Yes. For some reason her mother had been led to believe, or wished to believe, in some more permanent arrangement. Perhaps she began to make demands and things were getting out of hand. Certainly her expectations were echoed by Beattie. Literally. Think of it: a voluble, street-wise kid calling you "Dad"— can you imagine anything more threatening to a respectable man who's having an affair with a part-time prostitute?'

Annette concentrated for a while on eating her dinner in silence. Then she said, 'You're right. I'm not giving you an argument, not on this score, anyway. If he'd decided to dump her and she wouldn't let him—maybe she'd even found out something by then that made him vulnerable—his full name, where he worked, where he lived—then, yes, he's going to silence her. But, that's all in the past. Been and gone. How can it be relevant to what happened to Beattie?'

'Supposing—just supposing—that after all

these years she suddenly discovered the identity of the man who really did ruin her mother's life?'

'It's not impossible . . . But how?'

'Dunno. She wants recompense, she's entitled to it. But I don't believe she could set about it on her own; she hadn't the background, the education, the confidence. Putting all that aside—even if she was capable of approaching this man—she might have been afraid, felt in need of protection. After all, he almost killed her mother. So she'd need someone to help her.'

They looked at each other for some moments in silence. Annette said, expressionlessly, 'Reggie.'

'Why not?'

'Liz, were you sitting there in the Railway putting this together in your head?'

'Yes. Shut up. Listen. You've no idea how quixotic Reggie was, how gallant. If a woman went to him with a story like that, it wouldn't matter what sort of a woman she was—he'd do his best to help her.'

'But why approach *him*—and why should he help her?'

'Because there's a single answer to both those questions. He knew who the man was.'

'I need another drink.'

'You never knew Reggie. If someone said to him—there's been a terrible injustice, you have the means to help to put it right—then he'd feel it was his duty, simple humanity.'

'Forgive me, Liz. Everybody, up to this point, including you, has given me the impression that Reggie wasn't capable of doing his own thinking. Now, suddenly, according to you, he's efficiently going about fixing, organising . . . What in God's name has this to do with meetings at bus stops and whisking this woman off Christ knows where— which is no more than a lot of silly farting about.'

'It was. You're right, you've just said it. Someone was telling him what to think, what to do—and no matter how fartingly silly, he'd do it. Then . . . it might be difficult to approach this man, it might have needed tact, cunning, time . . . anything. So they had to plan, make arrangements. He could still be dangerous, couldn't he? Threatened—perhaps with exposure, after all these years when he thought he'd got away with it. You said—we've only had Doris's version. There must be police records, they might tell us something different—they'd certainly tell us more. There could even be some possible clue to his identity.'

'Liz, the police records won't exist any more. At least, I doubt it very much, not an incident like that—as Doris said, they're ten a penny round here.'

Liz was looking at her in amazement. 'Do you mean—you don't keep records?'

185

'Yes, but not necessarily for very long. There's no legal requirement X number of years, depends entirely on Force policy. It's only unsolved murders that are never thrown away and that wasn't murder, it was assault occasioning actual bodily harm. No, you're going up a blind alley with that one.'

'Doesn't matter. I'll have to think of something else.' She sat concentrating, her face very determined. 'He'd be quite an age now, possibly retired. At the time he wasn't a boy, or a young man—he was mature, I'm sure he was from the way Doris spoke about him.'

'Don't forget she was looking with a child's eyes. Everyone out of their teens is ancient.'

'I know. But a very young man can change a great deal over the years—almost out of recognition. An older man, though, given ten, twenty years—'

'Nearer thirty.'

'O.K. But you see what I'm getting at. He's greyer, he stoops a bit, he's put on weight, but when Beattie saw his face . . . she'd see the man she wanted to call Dad.'

'Meanwhile,' Annette made an effort to sound sensible. She had an uncomfortable feeling that what Liz lacked in training and professional expertise, she made up for with intuition. Supposing she was right? 'Meanwhile, there's this mysterious third party behind the scenes, directing everything.'

'Mmm.'

186

They were both silent for a while, thinking. Annette folded her napkin. Folded it again. This was going to be difficult.

'Yes?' Liz was watching her.

'You loved Reggie. You need to prove his innocence. You're a nice girl, and you're highly intelligent. Every step along this way you're establishing his association with Beattie—something he denied to us, to his sister. But now you've managed to turn him into a white knight, coming to the aid of a damsel in distress. Are you sure you're not doing this because it's the only way you can live with his memory?'

'I don't know, Annette. I don't know.'

*   *   *

She lay awake long into the night, her brain refusing to wind down. She fell asleep at last and woke late, stupefied, unable to make sense of anything.

To clear her mind she went for a hurtling bicycle ride, coming home, keyed-up, to begin a manic house blitz—working from the kitchen to the sitting room, cleaning, vacuuming, rearranging. After a pause for a quick lunch, she flung herself back into her housework and then, in the sitting room, taking the cushion from one of the armchairs, she came to a halt. Puzzled at first, then, after a moment, shocked, staring, motionless.

187

When the phone rang she jumped, having no idea how long she had been standing staring at the object she had placed on a side table.

'Liz, it's Arabella. About your bloody chair.'

Arabella. Chair. Liz was making connections only slowly. Arabella had a workshop in Hambling, specialising in furniture restoration. 'Chair . . .'

'Oh, Liz, you promised to collect it last week. I know you've been having a rotten time lately, ducky, and I do sympathise—but I need the *space.*'

. . . a Victorian mahogany chair she had bought cheap because it was a singleton and the seat was wrecked. '*That* chair.'

'Give the girl a banana. *That* chair.'

Liz apologised, still dazed by her discovery, certain only of one thing: that she must go to Hunter with it. She explained she would stop off on her way into Chatfield—'about fifteen minutes.'

Which was how she came to be trapped, with no hope of escape, loading the chair into the back of her car. Paula appeared beside her. 'Here, let me give you a hand. Push this way . . .'

They managed it between them; Liz with the conviction she would have expended a great deal less energy if she'd been left to do it alone.

Paula was pleased. 'Good job I was here to

help. Come and have a cup of tea.'

'I'm sorry, I—'

'Come on, I need to talk. You're not one to bear a grudge.' She looked so woebegone, shabby and bedraggled, her face greasy. Liz, about to refuse, hesitated. It was too late then. Paula said, 'Good, come on.

'O.K. But I really haven't got time to go back to your place. Let's nip into the caff on the corner. I'll pay.'

It was a cheap, plastic place, not somewhere she would normally have chosen. But it was close by, and anything was better than being dragged back into Paula's manic kitchen. When they had got their tea, a huge slice of cake for Paula, and were sitting down, Liz said, 'What grudge do you mean?'

'I know the funeral was difficult—my nerves, I was so traumatised, finding Reggie's body. I don't think I was altogether fair, saying that about your mother not being closely related and everything.'

'Let's forget it, Paula. It was a bad time for both us.'

'Well, I think that's the point, it couldn't possibly be as bad for you as for me. Things sort of just roll off you, you don't take them to heart—but he *was* my *brother* and I have to live the rest of my life knowing he's marked down as a self-confessed murderer.'

'Paula, that's just not true.'

'What—that you don't take things to heart?'

'Oh, shut up, of course I do. He didn't do it, Paula, *that's* not true—'

Paula looked at her blankly. 'But you said—his suicide note—we agreed—you agreed—'

'I know I did. At the time I was so overwhelmed I couldn't think straight. I can now. His alibi, he couldn't *possibly* have done it if he was the other side of Cheshire, we forgot that, we didn't take it into account under the stress of the moment. I can think more clearly now, even if you're too obviously upset to. None of us, none of us, have to live with that awful . . . *acceptance*. I'm going to see to it we don't. I'm going to find out who did it. Paula, you're spilling your tea.'

Paula ignored the dribbling cup. When she found her voice she said, 'You don't mean . . . You don't mean you know who it was.'

'Not yet, but I will.' She reached across the table, firmly put the cup down in the swilling saucer.

'But . . . how? If the police . . .'

'They're *wrong*. Get that into your head. And I'm going to prove it to them.'

Paula sounded bewildered. 'But they've closed the case. They won't listen to you, will they?'

'If they don't, I'll just carry on.'

Paula sat back, frowning. 'Carry on with what? I mean, have you got clues and things?'

'Well, not exactly . . .' Caution. If she said too much Paula would go rushing off to Helen

190

who was beginning to find her emotional balance again. And there was something else. For the first time the importance of secrecy occurred to Liz; Annette's professional discretion would protect her theory—give it to Paula and before the day was out everyone in Hambling would know that Liz was on the track of a murderer living undiscovered *in their very midst* . . .

'Not exactly . . .' Paula, staring at her intently, reverted to her combative self. 'Oh, don't think I can't see what you're up to. Helen and I have been through a traumatic experience and you can't stand being out of the limelight, can you? Honestly, you're so *childish.* You always want Helen to be looking at you, taking notice of you—you'd say anything—'

'I haven't said a *word* of this to her, and *don't you.* It would be cruel to raise her hopes before I have proof, or at least something more positive—

Liz was trying to hang on to her patience, but she was aware their voices were rising. In her present state Paula could work up into an instant blazing scene and it would be all over Hambling, with someone only too eager to carry news of it to Helen before the shouting had died down.

'So *childish,*' Paula said again. 'So transparently childish. Helen's always said you do the wrong thing for the right reasons—I suppose you think that's what you're doing now. Well, you're not—you're just wrong all the way. You're trying to be clever. And you're trying to impress her—What's it going to be like for her with you going about on all this cloak and dagger nonsense—'

Liz kept her voice low, but forceful. 'I told you. She knows absolutely nothing about it and I don't intend—'

'She'd be so *upset*—you getting the family talked about. She ought to be told, she ought to know—'

'Paula, you're not listening—'

'You bloody listen. If there'd been the least suspicion falling on anyone *else*—I'd have been the one to know about it. There's very little goes on in Hambling I don't hear about—you're not here half the time, what can you find out? But me, I keep my ear to the ground—'

Pity someone doesn't stamp on your head. Me, for instance. If the price of peace was letting Paula exercise her scorn, she'd bite her tongue and let her get on with it.

'—I mean, are you going to go around asking for everyone's *alibi*? Well, I'll give you mine here and now. And what about your own, eh? Eh? You were very mysteriously missing that weekend—'

'Paula, don't be ridiculous—'

'You're the one whose going to make herself ridiculous—going around with your

192

magnifying glass and deerstalker—'

'I don't need this. I have to go, anyway, I have an appointment.'

It wasn't; it was an errand. She wasn't looking forward to it but it certainly gave her a great deal of savage satisfaction to keep its purpose from Paula.

CHAPTER EIGHTEEN

Hunter had a Senior Officers' meeting just about to start—'I'm sorry, Liz, it's lovely to see you but I'm terribly pushed. I can only spare you ten minutes.'

Liz, moving from foot to foot like an awkward schoolgirl, said, 'I'm not sure you will be pleased. But it is important.'

'Sit down, let's make a start, then we'll see where we can take it. I'm not letting you walk out of here now.'

She drew the bracelet from an envelope, where she had placed it, wrapped in tissue paper, not wanting to handle it directly. 'After I went back to school, at the beginning of September, I discovered—when I came home at weekends—that Reggie had been—entertaining someone in my house. He knew where the key was hidden. He thought I wouldn't mind. It only happened a few times, always on a Thursday night. I never knew who the person was. This morning, I was having a blitz—cleaning, tidying. In one of the armchairs in the sitting room, tucked down by the side of the cushion, I found this.'

She put the packet on his desk. He sat unmoving, big, capable hands clasped. She leaned forward, opened the paper, fingers trembling slightly. She had never before experienced silence of such density. 'You see, it's a bracelet. They've been all the rage recently, I've had to confiscate one or two from the girls at school, they're not allowed jewellery, well, not during class . . .' She swore at herself under her breath to stop talking drivel. 'The thing about these . . .' It was a gaudy object, flimsy and rattling. She spread it flat. 'You see—they have initials worked into the design—er—the owner's initials.'

After what seemed a long silence, he took a pencil, moved the bracelet with it, said, 'B.B.'

'Yes. Please believe me, I never, never thought, for one moment, that the woman he was entertaining was Beattie.'

'But you were in possession of that information, and you withheld it. Do you realise what it would have meant at that stage of the investigation, how much work it would have saved—and how it would have influenced the outcome? Yes . . . I could have used it to fight the old man to keep the investigation open.'

She couldn't allow herself to think of the

significance of that. She could only think she had been waiting for his fury to fall on her and now that it had it was all the more unnerving for being so controlled . . .

He said, 'I'm going to keep this,' picked up the phone, said something curt and incomprehensible into it about an entry in something that seemed to be called the other-than-found-property book. Turned back to her. 'Well, girl? What else?'

How did he *know*? 'I went to the Railway last night and talked to Doris.'

Amazement displaced everything. 'What in God's name for?'

'Because I knew that if I spoke to her, woman to woman, I'd find something out. I did. It's too complicated to tell you now, but, er . . . Oh, and Annette came with me. You *mustn't* be angry with her.' She was quite confident of coming between Annette and his wrath, at least for the present, knowing that Annette had that very morning begun several days' leave, off to visit her parents. 'She tried to talk me out of it, I had to persuade her. She didn't want me going there on my own.'

'Oh, God—' whatever he had been about to say, the phone interrupted him. He grabbed it up, listened, barked, 'Straight away,' crashed it back. He stood up. 'Come on, I'll see you off the premises, I don't want you hanging round here suborning my staff.' Then they were striding down a corridor and she had to skip to

195

keep up with him. He said, 'I'll be tied up till about five or six, I'll phone you. I'll see you this evening. Don't say you're busy. We have to talk. And I'll have calmed down by then.' He held a door open, stood unmoving. 'Now, go away, girl, before I charge you with something. Anything. The mood I'm in I'm not fussy.'

*   *   *

She jumped when the phone rang at 6.30. Tried to gauge the tone of his, 'Hallo, Liz.'

'How are you?' she asked diffidently.

'Clothed and in my right mind.'

A pause, then her sudden laughter. Thank God, she wasn't going to spend the evening being wretched and apologising for her existence.

He arranged to pick her up. She had expected some local pub; no, it was Stavely Manor. She had to rush upstairs, start throwing clothes about. Stavely was Helen's favourite place, it was where they'd gone the day she'd come rushing back from school after Paula's phone call, to find Helen making a bonfire in the back garden.

The luxury of Stavely was restrained by perfect taste. There could not be an atmosphere smoother, more restful. Hunter looked impressive, expensively tailored; he was discreetly addressed by name. She wondered if

196

he was often there, with whom. She said, 'If I make a kind of comprehensive apology now, will that do? I really mean it. Helen's always saying I do the wrong thing for the right reason.'

He had to sledgehammer his thoughts to order. She sat exquisitely opposite him in a narrow amber silk dress that followed every supple movement of her body; silver belt and sandals and bangles; he had never seen pearls look voluptuous before, as they did against her skin.

'Er—so you're going to tell me now—what you've done and why?'

'Well . . . not instantly. Do you mind if I just give my attention to this marvellous menu? You see, I have a theory and it's going to take quite a lot of explaining.'

'Of course. A theory . . .' He managed to look interested and not condescending. When, eventually, mellowed by wine, delicious food and charmingly inconsequential conversation, she did tell him, he gave her a long, careful look.

She heard again in her head all her arguments: muddled, inconclusive. 'I haven't made sense, have I?'

'I didn't say that. Let's go through it systematically. From the beginning—for you that's when you found out Reggie was using your house to—entertain someone. You must have spoken to him about it.'

'Only in a general way. I didn't want to pry. I said I'd rather he didn't do it again—you know the sort of thing.'

'No, I don't. As far as I'm concerned your entire family are straight out of P. G. Wodehouse —how do I know how you speak to one another?'

She swallowed a giggle. Could he possibly mean it?

'You said—it was always on a Thursday. Did he tell you that?'

'Oh, gosh, no, he didn't really tell me anything. He was awfully evasive—secretive. If you'd known him, he could talk for ages and say absolutely nothing. No, I worked it out, it was simple enough. The dustbin's emptied on a Thursday morning—there was always a wine bottle in it on Friday.' She felt the incongruity of talking about dustbins in the most expensive restaurant for miles around. If he found it exceptional he gave no indication, perhaps his life was constantly ambushed by such mundane matters.

'So—he went to Cheltenham. You came to see me and I told you Beattie's name. Surely you asked him then if he knew her?'

'Well, no, I never had the chance. You see, I'd been away for a fortnight, which was unusual. The weekend I *didn't* come home was when it all happened, so when I did come back to Hambling a week later Reggie had become very upset about the situation, actually it had made him quite ill. On the day he left for Cheltenham, he—um—he wouldn't see me.' She was silent for a space. It had hurt her to say it, but she knew she had to be truthful.

'Then—' he prompted quietly.

Her long, fine fingers fiddled with the stem of her wine glass. 'Then, yes. This is difficult because I'm breaking a promise. I swore to Helen I would never speak of this—I really did think when it happened that you should know but . . . she was so embarrassed, so shocked, it was really humiliating for her. That day I came to see you at Hambling, I spent the evening at Woodside. Two of Helen's friends came round, we played whist. Very soon after they'd left, about a quarter to eleven, there was a ring at the front door . . .' She told him about the lay-figure in the porch.

He did a double-take. For once, she'd astonished him. 'An inflatable . . .'

'Yes. Gruesome, nasty. I can't tell you what it was like trying to explain it to Helen.'

'Did she understand?'

'Well, she understood *something*, I'm not quite sure what. Oh, it's all right, I know it's funny in a ghastly way. At the time I had to calm her down, reassure her, so . . .' She explained how she had disposed of it the following morning. He sat back, shaking his head, but before he could speak she said, 'I know, I know, it was wrong. But you have no idea what sort of a state Helen was in—and she was convinced it was someone malicious, playing this cruel trick . . . I must admit I agreed with her then—now, I can see—

'Yes, we'll come to that, let's keep this in sequence.'

'Oh, I see, yes. I insisted then that Reggie must come back from Cheltenham—if she was being persecuted, she needed his protection. That was the way I saw it,' she gave a short, bitter laugh. 'There I was, at it again—the wrong thing for the right reasons. Because he came home, and he killed himself. At least, to all appearances—but you know I won't accept that. So what I did, after his funeral, I went round all the neighbours closest to Helen and asked them if they'd seen anyone—anyone at all going into Woodside the morning Reggie died.' She paused and looked at him challengingly. 'Are you going to say I shouldn't have done?'

'You can do what you want with your own time. You're not interfering with any on-going investigation. You're being very determined and resourceful. No, Liz, there's no need to be defensive. Go on.'

'Well, there's a family recently moved three doors down. Of course, they were all out except Mrs Maltravers, but I had a good talk with her. She saw someone going down the pathway at the end of the gardens—later on that same morning.'

'Someone?'

200

'Yes. She thought it was the old boy who always walks there twice a day—but it was too late for him. As she's new she didn't realise he had set times. I went to see his daughter, just to make sure he hadn't altered them or anything, and she told me he's been away—at his son's since before Reggie died. So it couldn't have been him.'

'I'll hand it to you, you've gone about this really thoroughly, and I don't want to discourage you, but . . . You said this woman lives three houses away. On an ordinary road that's nothing—in Woodside it could be a mile. Somebody going down the back could be going anywhere. Turning off before they reached your aunt's. Man or woman?'

'She couldn't tell—she just assumed it was a man because she assumed it was Mr Truelove—but it was a glimpse of someone across a distance, and all covered up in waterproofs. But there is a back way to Helen's, you have to know about it because it's not obvious—although even if you didn't know, if you were really looking, you'd find it. But it did occur to me—the person who dumped that ghastly lay-figure might have come in the back way. I did go and have a look—the morning after that episode, but how could I tell? I don't know how to recognise clues and things.'

'You're doing damn well, girl. So, after seeing the neighbours, you went along to the

Railway and spoke to Doris. Woman to woman.' He was so obviously taken with the notion she looked at him defensively until he added, 'That must have been quite something.' What he was thinking—he couldn't say—Liz and Annette, shining in that scuffed, workaday place . . .

As a matter of fact, she was really nice. And I thought she was very perceptive.' She told him, briefly, what Doris had to say about the meeting, then about what had happened to Beattie's mother. 'You didn't know about her, did you?'

'No, I didn't. And I must admit it's a new idea a third party introducing them.' The woman in Katie's Kaff with Beattie . . . there was no reason to assume a connection, but the time fitted. 'And that brings us up to today—finding the bracelet.' Beattie had told people her mystery man took her somewhere 'ever so nice'. He thought of Liz's house: the bend in the lane, the sheltering trees and high hedges; geographically, no house could be more disposed for secrecy. He thought how beautiful he had found it—to Beattie it would have been heaven. George Wither's original impression had been that Reggie had taken Beattie to the posh house with the garden big enough for a swimming pool—that would have to be revised, the description certainly didn't fit Liz's. And perhaps he had just shown her, described it . . . And they had always taken it for granted that the house was in Hambling, but now, that might not necessarily be the case. It could be in the surrounding area, anywhere and—a startling possibility—lived in by the man who had attempted to kill Beattie's mother. 'We don't know why he took her to your house. According to your theory they planned strategy over a bottle of wine. But isn't that overlooking the obvious? I know she was blowsy and common—but men are men— that could have been the type that turned him on. That's not something he'd be likely to tell you, is it?'

'No. I'm not saying there wasn't an element of sex—well, maybe sexual attraction, but I don't think it ever went beyond that.' She had all too often doubted that Reggie had ever had it in his life, but it would be the ultimate betrayal to say so. 'Reggie was easily flattered in the first place. If she was presentable and appealed to his gallantry, he could have been attracted to her. As for not being seen about with her in Hambling—I can think of two good reasons. First, he wouldn't want word to get back to Helen he was being seen about with a bit of a tart. Second, we don't know what sort of contact, if any, they'd made with this man— the man who had behaved so brutally to Beattie's mother. It might have been necessary for them to lie low for a certain time. Maybe *never* reveal themselves, just make Beattie's demands and then . . .'

203

She looked lost, she hadn't thought beyond that point.

'Take the money and run.'

'Well, that would be the whole point, wouldn't it?'

He was not so sure, but nothing in his attitude indicated this. She was giving him a great deal more to think about than she realised. 'Have you done anything else?'

She was abstracted. 'Such as?'

'The way you're carrying on it could be anything.'

She gazed at him blankly for a moment, then shrugged. 'What else is there to do? I've thought and I've thought and I have a feeling—no, I don't have any evidence—that it all started out as a bit of a lark for him, then it got out of hand. Maybe he wanted to back out and found he couldn't. He might not have been told the whole truth of the situation in the first place.'

'Beattie was a pretty tough customer. She'd had to fight for her existence since she was a kid. He wouldn't have been a match for her if she decided to cut up rough.'

'No . . . That last evening. I know Reggie so well, how he behaved when he'd got himself into a jam. He'd just take himself out of the way, mess about. He really, really believed that if he made himself scarce, by the time he surfaced again the situation would have put itself right. I'm convinced that's what he was doing that night, standing Beattie up, getting as far away as possible. Look, the anonymous phone call—he kept his meetings with her secret—but that person knew. Why *do* people make anonymous calls?'

'All sorts of reasons. Sheer malice. Reggie's name would have to be known to this person but there need be absolutely no other connection—just someone with a mental kink wanting to make mischief. Someone with a grudge against him—it could be for something absolutely trivial—again malicious enough to want to cause him embarrassment. Someone not necessarily guilty of anything who stands to lose by being implicated in some way— therefore lands him firmly in it before he can defend himself. An accomplice—same reason, strike first and shove it all on Reggie. Or . . . the murderer, to save his skin.'

She was listening to him very carefully; at this she nodded. 'This man they were tracking down. *If* they'd revealed themselves to him, he could know quite a bit about them—their movements, their arrangements. He could have been the one Beattie was with that night—the one who murdered her.'

He had given a great deal of thought to this, several steps ahead of her. 'You could very well be right.'

'But I can't think now, what else to do, where else to go.'

'That's just as well. Leave it now, Liz.

You've been very thorough, leave it to me now. No, I'm not promising anything, I couldn't at this stage, I need to turn things over in my mind. Anyway, you'll be back at school next week, won't you?'

'Yes.'

Out of harm's way. A very unpleasant possibility had been growing on him. For the present, he filed it away in the corner of his mind. 'How much of this did you tell Annette?'

'Just my theory—about Beattie finding the man—'

'Not about the lay-figure—or your enquiries round the neighbours?'

'No. And obviously not the bracelet because I only found it today. Why?'

'It's just,' he said with grim politeness, 'that I do like to be one step ahead of my staff.'

CHAPTER NINETEEN

Over the weekend Liz stayed with Helen at Woodside. It was what they both needed, to be quietly together. Friends, relatives, acquaintances; dear, vague Uncle William— all had returned to their everyday concerns.

Liz suggested Saturday shopping in Hambling; Helen said, 'You go, darling, meet your friends for coffee and gossip.'

Liz would not sink to the blackmailing

simplicity of *I'm not going without you.* She had a suspicion that Helen had not been into Hambling since Reggie's funeral—which to Liz was entirely understandable. She was young and tough and had learnt how to outstare anyone; Helen was made of more fragile stuff, her grief deeper. She would need time to re-encounter the faces, the routines she and Reggie had taken for granted all their adult lives. So Liz suggested Chester. It took no more than token persuasion.

The afternoon drive home gave her time to consider. There were things she needed to speak to Helen about, delicate and difficult ground to cover. She had to make a start somewhere. 'I was at Stavely yesterday evening, with Mr Hunter.' Helen said how nice, darling, looking politely at a loss, so Liz had to remind her who Hunter was. When this registered, Helen asked in a baffled way, 'Why on earth did you do that?'

'He asked me,' Liz said reasonably.

'Oh . . . You must think me stupid, what a *crass* question. Of course he would want to take you out. He's very attractive, mature . . . Not married?'

'Divorced.'

'Ah . . .'

It made Liz smile. Helen needed the merest dulcet exclamation to convey how very sensible it was of Hunter to be single and to have the good taste to take her to Stavely. And, um, we did have things to talk about.' When Helen let this pass without any comment for some time, Liz prompted gently. 'Helen . . . About Reggie.'

Helen sounded tired. 'So I assume. I'd rather leave it, for the present.

Hurriedly—*oh, yes, of course . . . it can wait* . . . The coward's way out. Although, driving through the damp, shrouded Cheshire lanes was not the best time for a serious talk. She would have to make sure the weekend did not slip past taking the right moment with it; she was not the only person who knew about Reggie's meeting with Beattie—other people, unnumbered, unknown, also knew. It could only be a matter of time before word got round to Helen. *I have to be the one to tell her.*

But left to her own thoughts, she was free to recall the end of her evening with Hunter. On the drive home he told her he would be away over the weekend, in the Lake District, walking with friends; they went regularly, stayed in a cottage with no telephone. When he saw her to her door, he seemed to be inwardly absorbed with some problem. He said, 'I'd like to see you again, please. Next weekend. Shall I phone you when you come home?'

She said yes, please, and he took both her hands. 'You'll be safely tucked away in Surrey next week. Don't do anything in the meanwhile, will you? I'm not sure I'm happy about being away and you here on the loose.'

'I'll be staying with Helen at Woodside.'

'Good,' he sounded relieved, absently kissed her cheek. 'Take care of yourself, girl.'

*   *   *

Tea in front of the fire seemed to Liz the best moment. Helen had planned the evening: a quiet supper, then the Dalrymples for whist. Liz, visited by a lightning-flash of the lay-figure, streaming and obscene in the porch after the last whist evening, marvelled at Helen's fortitude. It was that decided her.

'Helen—I know this is difficult, but if we could just have a few words now, then we can talk more—or not—as you please. There's something I have to say to you because I feel it's dishonest of me to know something about Reggie that you should know.'

Helen said nothing. She sat in her armchair, the fine china saucer restful in her hands; she was gazing at the fire. Liz thought—is she listening? 'It's always been understood between us that Reggie's apology in his last note was for causing you distress. We never believed he had anything to do with Beattie. I'm afraid we were wrong. The police have found an eye-witness to their meeting. It was in a pub in Chatfield in the summer and—and there were other occasions . . .' Not my house, you don't need to know that; the house you

209

bought me, that he used . . . Helen's lack of response was unnerving. 'You do understand I had to tell you. The police know, other people—it's the kind of thing that you want to be kept quiet but becomes common knowledge. Sooner or later Paula's bound to get to know and it would be—'

Helen turned a calm face to her. That she was suffering was evident; but there was no shock, no rejection. 'I knew there had to be something like that. Waiting to be found out.'

Liz stared at her, dumb.

'My dear, I've known him all my life. I knew he was lying to me. I asked him, and he lied. Not because he'd done anything wrong, but because he was ashamed of the type of woman he'd chosen to associate with.'

Liz found her voice. 'Nobody knows what their exact relationship was . . . Perhaps some ill-advised flirtation . . . As for him *choosing* to associate with her—I think he was somehow, goodness knows how, inveigled into well, say, taking her out, giving her money. I think he'd very soon change his mind, try to call it all off—but if she was perhaps overbearing, determined to hang on to him . . .' Liz stumbled on, feeling the burden of knowledge of so many things and the necessity of keeping them from Helen.

The instinct to protect, colliding with the desire to comfort, produced a confusion from which, amazingly, a new thought emerged.

Beattie might not *just* have been using him to hunt down the man who had wrecked her mother's life. She might have been threatening him. 'Helen, she could have been blackmailing him, not necessarily for money, but to maintain the relationship—'

'I've thought of that. I've thought of everything since he died. *Knowing*, knowing this detail or that, this reason or that, isn't going to bring him back. When he denied all knowledge of that woman—just for an instant—I believed him. Then I knew it wasn't true. But I never, for one moment, let him know that. He needed my love, my good opinion; I thought that by letting him keep his deception I was helping him. Even though he was driven to such a dreadful act of despair, his comfort would be that I believed in him.'

For a moment, Liz wondered if Helen had been under so much strain she was not, temporarily, as mentally stable as she should be. Then she saw how necessary it was—this painful double-think. Helen had been building resolution to carry her into the future; she found it in the conviction that she had not let her brother down.

Liz thought, I can't cope with this. Only she had to, and there was no easy way of saying it. 'There's an assumption—people—not everyone —some people think Reggie's suicide was an act of remorse. His good name, his memory, is tarnished. We can't allow—'

'Liz, you're getting into such a coil about this. You've just given a very good reason why he could be guilty. Victims frequently kill their blackmailers, I believe.'

Liz, mortified, feeling twelve years old, understanding nothing, incapable of looking beyond the limits of her own absurd assumptions, sat in silence.

'No, of course he's not guilty—we know that, the people who care about him know that. What on earth does it matter about anyone else? Ignorant, spiteful, credulous people are going to say what they're going to say and no amount of evidence or proof will stop them. Darling, I understand your idealism, I would expect no less of you. But the important thing now is to rebuild our lives, not—keep returning to this—picking it over—'

'This is awful—as if I'm some kind of— vulture. I just truly, truly believe there's a way of proving him innocent, if only—'

'Vulture, nonsense. I know your motives are of the best, they do you credit.' Helen reached out, took her hand and held it. 'Liz, I am so *tired* of trying to make sense of this. For my sake, for his sake, let him rest in peace, in the peace of our love.'

She agreed, of course, the emotional pressure was irresistible. Evening, supper, whist with the Dalrymples . . . It was *almost* as if nothing had ever happened, and before she went to sleep in the room at Woodside that was always 'Liz's room' she thought again of how unfeeling she had been to try to deprive Helen of comfort. If Helen wanted to draw a line under everything, then, that was what she must do. And Sheldon had insisted, too—*leave it now, Liz.* Perhaps . . . the faint hope stirred; perhaps, given time, Helen might feel differently. But at least they'd got it all said and done, it wasn't going to hang over her for the rest of the weekend.

*   *   *

Sunday was a silver-gilt morning, the fields quilted with frost, spiders' webs on hawthorn bushes crystallised to white lace. They went for a drive, then coffee at Midham with Robert and his father; it did Helen good to be with them, they were very gallant with her and unfailingly loyal to Reggie.

Back at Woodside, after lunch, Liz read the papers lazily in front of the fire while Helen rested. They were to entertain friends to tea and when Liz at last roused herself to make preparations it was to discover there was no ice cream. There was everything else: minuscule triangular sandwiches—egg, salmon, cucumber—crustless. Slender wedges of delicious quiche. Scones and raspberry jam and cream. Melting almond slices. The heirloom Richelieu tablecloth, fine as a cobweb, every piece of china transparent as a sea shell. But no ice cream. Helen said it really didn't matter, but Liz knew how much it meant to her to do everything properly. 'You know people always expect Bellamy's ice cream when they come to Hambling. It's unthinkable not to at least offer it. I insist on going.' It would take her no more than twenty minutes, there was plenty of time.

The early darkness was closing in, shrouded by fog; it was bitterly cold. The lights of Bellamy's shone warmly across the market square; famous for their home-made ice cream and chocolates, they stayed open on a Sunday all year, even though in winter there were few tourists about.

Impelled by the thought of guests imminent, Liz rushed in, found herself standing at the counter beside the egregious Melanie Beadnall.

Liz was damned if she would do more than nod hallo; then there was nothing for it but to stick it out—out of season, no one hurried. Mr Bellamy was in the back, finding something for a patient customer; Mrs Bellamy generally *had her leg*, served everyone at snail's pace and went away frequently to sit down. Presumably now.

At once, Melanie began to talk. She had a quick, soft voice, rushing in and out of giggles; a limpet persistence, pressing ideas, diets, homeopathic remedies, entire modes of life upon people. Rather like Paula. They lived in houses facing across Victoria Square, sat on the same committees, did conspicuous things at the same demonstrations. Loathed one another.

Liz heard, torrentially, that Mummy was just out of hospital *at last*, you can't keep a good girl down—and we're just on our way now to Pamela's—she's having the kiddies—school, you know—then Trevor and I are off to spend a few days with Mummy, soothing the invalid's fevered brow . . .

Liz was by now accustomed to people being embarrassed in her presence; Reggie's name (Murderer! Suicide!) shrieked unspoken.

'. . . and of course, *daren't go* without Bellamy's chocs. More than my life's worth . . .'

Perhaps because Liz yawned; perhaps because time waited excruciatingly to be filled and Melanie had exhausted the minutiae of her family's doings . . . Amongst a rush of giggles, Melanie said, 'Er, it was terrible. I'm sorry about—er—Reggie.'

'Yes,' Liz said neutrally. She knew the giggles were embarrassment but she could scarcely be expected to join in.

'It was odd—seeing her, but of course, everyone said after he was arrest—when he was—um—that he didn't *know* her, so who was I to—You know, DAC.'

Liz glanced sideways, down at the pink, working face. Did it matter what she was dribbling about? An instinct alerted her: it did.

'*You* know, the scheme for developing

Chatfield and surrounding areas. Paula and I are on the committee—well, *were*, Paula's not any more, you know her—always other irons in the fire—' An indulgent laugh. 'Well, it looked like her, from those posters they displayed, but as I wasn't sure . . .'

Liz was trying to put this into sense; she was beginning to grasp what Melanie was saying. There was a slight commotion of movement from the back of the shop coinciding—from outside—with the pip-pip-pip of a car horn.

'Oh, gosh, Trevor—the kiddies—mother's chocs—' Melanie craned this way and that; the delay was not her fault but Trevor was the kind of man who punished his wife for his own impatience. 'And, I mean, she hardly looked the type to be interested in civic affairs, but it takes all sorts, I always say. Of course, I couldn't hear what she was saying but she certainly spent enough time on that fascinating display of—Oh, Mrs Bellamy, thank you—

Fumblings, purse, money, while Liz's mind crashed into gear. Last summer. The exhibition in the shopping mall in Chatfield. Paula—bossing. Reggie and Wilfred—helpers: carrying, setting up stands . . . 'Melanie, do you mean this woman was—you saw her with Reggie?'

'Well, she was at your stand and—'

Rattling. Trevor rapping on shop door.

—*you utter nerd, why don't you just open it*—

Mrs Bellamy, limping, puzzled. 'Is it locked?

We don't close till—'

Melanie juggled chocolates, handbag, gloves. 'No, Mrs Bellamy, it's just my—men are so—aren't they?'

'Melanie—'

'Sorry, Liz, must fly.'

Liz drove back to Woodside trying to make something of it all. Melanie was famously silly, which made it all the more unlikely she would be capable of fabricating the incident. No, it had happened. But what did it mean?

Back at Woodside the guests had arrived. Tea was a ceremonially social occasion, and a delight to Helen's heart. It meant a great deal to Liz to be instrumental in it; she put aside her attacks of conscience as she went to the phone time and again, with a medley of excuses, trying to get hold of Paula. She tried after the guests had gone, during supper, when the Dalrymples arrived for whist. At one point she took the opportunity to say to Helen, 'The weekend's wonderfully clear of Paula. Do you know where she's gone?'

'I'm just thanking heaven it's *somewhere.*'

'Oh, absolutely.' Bugger Paula. The only time one had something to say to her she couldn't be found.

She went back to the card game, the ivory and gold of the drawing room, the gently enfolding evening. She would try later when she was in her own house. Then, well . . . she would just have to leave it.

CHAPTER TWENTY

Rcalling Paula's truculence last time they met, Liz decided to by-pass her and telephone Hunter. It was two days before she could reach him. 'I don't want to be a nuisance,' Liz said, 'but I've found out something.'

'Liz, you promised me you wouldn't do anything.'

'I didn't, I didn't. I stood next to a woman in a shop. That's not doing anything, is it?'

He laughed, resigned. 'All right.'

'Her name's Melanie Beadnall—' Briefly, Liz explained Melanie and her circumstances. 'I saw her on Sunday but she dashed off before I could get anything much out of her. What it is—you know there's a development scheme for Chatfield and surrounding areas, Hambling included. Last summer there was an exhibition in that big new shopping mall in Chatfield—all sorts of people were represented, historical societies, environmentalists, residents' associations—'

A wave of bafflement, eloquent as words.

'I know this seems utterly irrelevant but honestly, it's not. Paula was on the committee—well, she's on anything with the word "action" in it. She was mostly concerned with a display to do with Hambling— Hambling as it was, traditions, shops, buildings, businesses—you know the sort of thing.'

'Yes,' Hunter said patiently.

'This ghastly Melanie—'

'You didn't say she was ghastly.'

'Well, she is—she's on the committee, too. She was at the exhibition that day and she said Beattie was there.'

After a momentary silence, Hunter said, 'Hardly Beattie's sort of thing.'

'Exactly. What Melanie implies was that she was talking to Reggie, or that she was *with* Reggie.'

'Hang on, Liz. What was he doing there?'

'Oh, he was always awfully good with all Paula's demonstrations and things—' She had to pause. The past came back in a rush: so many times, so many years. Reggie, cheerful and kind and funny—lifting, carrying, setting up, going for sandwiches and coffee, manning stalls without much idea of what he was doing . . .

'Yes?' Hunter prompted gently.

'Er—yes. Helping. So that's why he would have been there, and I've been thinking about it, and when it was. Wilfred helped, too. They had rather a mad time, like a couple of schoolboys.'

'Wilfred?'

'An old friend of ours. He lives in Hampshire but he was up here last summer visiting his daughter.'

219

Hunter recalled the name, the photograph at Woodside—and hadn't Annette said he was at Reggie's funeral? 'But Melanie didn't specify who Beattie was talking to? It could have been Paula, or Reggie, or Wilfred.'

'Yes. I've been trying to work it out. We know why Reggie wouldn't mention it. And Wilfred, not being local he would never have seen those posters you put out after Beattie's death, and if he didn't know her name . . . But Paula . . .'

'What does she say?'

'I couldn't get hold of her on Sunday, and to be honest I haven't tried since. Last time I met her she behaved appallingly. I don't see why I should lay myself open to that again. I think the best way to approach this is through Melanie. Will you . . . will you go and see her? Ask her about it. Please?'

'Liz, this is pretty thin stuff.'

'I know, I know. But it's the *only* thing that's surfaced and—and it might lead somewhere.'

He didn't ask where. 'She might have made a mistake. She might have invented it.'

'Why should she?'

'People do.' A world of cynicism. And why did she tell you?'

Liz didn't have to think much about that. 'I'm sure she was just awkward, stuck next to me. I've got used to it over these months—people either go to any lengths to avoid mentioning Reggie or can't stop talking about him. I think she just said whatever came into her head and it was something that had actually happened.'

'All right. I'll drop in on her, I can't say when, and don't get your hopes up. I'll try and phone you Friday evening.'

'I'll be at Woodside, it'll be too difficult to say much.'

'Oh, well. I'll leave it till Saturday. At least I'll know you're with your aunt, not rushing around doing anything daft.' He gave her his private number—'in case you want to talk. And . . . I see Melanie, there's a trade-off.'

'What?'

'I take you out Saturday evening.'

She thought he was never going to get round to asking.

* * *

The Beadnalls' house in Victoria Square was gleamingly well-kept. Melanie looked at Hunter as if he had done something nasty in the porch, read his warrant card slowly, her expression pained. 'What do you want with me?'

Everything in her attitude told him she had been expecting him and he was the last person she wanted to see; she peered beyond him, avoiding his eyes. 'Just a few words, a matter of remembering something that happened in the summer. It would help us a great deal if you could spare a little time, but if you're busy I can come back later—perhaps when your husband's in?'

Alarm? Liz had the husband down as a total dork; Hunter wondered if he was bully, too. Melanie Beadnall said, 'Oh, very well.' She took him through to the kitchen where she busied herself unfolding a pile of ironing, refolding it garment by garment, carrying each separately to another part of the kitchen. This kept her continually on the move, too distracted by the importance of her task to give him more than minimal attention. As a defensive—or diversionary—tactic it had no effect on Hunter. He sat himself immovably at the kitchen table, ignored her comings and goings and took his time. The big country-style kitchen had all the appurtenances of contemporary living; Melanie was obviously a woman who safely did what everyone else did; had 2.4 children, a high fibre diet, the correct● wallpaper, pictures on the corkboard of baby seals being clubbed to death.

She faltered in her increasingly frantic activity to glance at him; he gave her a pleasant smile, saying nothing. She snapped, 'I can't think what I can tell you.'

'Oh, can't you?' he said cheerfully. 'It's about last summer's exhibition in the new shopping mall in Chatfield.'

She didn't wait for him to finish. 'I'm on the action committee, but if it's anything to do

222

with policy you'd better see our chairperson.'

'Oh, no, nothing like that. I understand that on one occasion during the exhibition, you identified the woman who in October was found—'

She moved out of his sight. He sat unmoving; her voice came to him, muttering. 'It's that Liz Farrell, I suppose. It was so *embarrassing* standing next to her in that shop. And she won't speak. Just stands there, absolute lamp post, looking superior . . . And all anyone can *think* of is that idiotic uncle of hers killing . . . I mean, I didn't say anything about *identifying* anyone. I just thought—she seemed to bear a resemblance—'

'Why don't you come and sit down and tell me all about it, and then I'll go away,' Hunter said comfortably.

She came cautiously into sight, crumpling something that looked like a vest in her restless hands. She knew when she was beaten. She sat down, sideways, on the edge of a chair, fixing a distraught gaze on the Aga.

'You were there, helping out on the stand . . .'

'Giving out leaflets, explaining what would happen if we let these bureaucratic vandals have their way, getting signatures for our petition . . . And this woman comes along. She was just looking as she passed, out of idle curiosity, not any sort of *commitment*. Anyone could tell civic awareness didn't come high on her agenda.'

'By "this woman" you mean the woman who was found drowned at Miller's Bridge—you recognised her later from the posters we put out?'

'Well . . . I can't be sure. It could have been her. I didn't take much notice, I was talking to a rather nice family who were very keen to support the protests, they had a couple of kiddies the same age as ours—I think it's so important to let kiddies know from a really early age that their voice counts in the community, don't you? Anyway, I was occupied but I couldn't help noticing she just came to a full stop further down the stand, just staring.'

'At what?' Hunter prompted, when Melanie paused. 'The display?'

'I—I couldn't really tell. Then Paula has to put her oar in. Miss Ego Trip. Ready to bore anyone to *death* with her family snaps.'

'Family snaps?'

'Well, all sorts, old Hambling . . . I mean, everyone contributed from their own collections. Lots of people have photographs of their forbears, it's very important to record social history in memorabilia like that. There was just about everything from around Hambling since photography was invented, people at their work, their leisure; weddings, funerals, family groups. And things like old bills and advertisements, pamphlets . . . all kinds.'

'And do you know what Paula's contribution was?'

'Huh, I wasn't interested. Not much as far as I could see. Some of her father's optician's shop on the High Street—I don't know what's so distinguished about being an optician. Some of the house as it used to be in the twenties or something, all the old codgers of relatives. But can you think of anything more naff than slipping in one taken recently—just because everyone's dressed in Edwardian clothes, tea in the garden or something. *I* think she was trying to pass it off as the real thing, only you could tell it wasn't because it was in colour. Everyone posing about dressed up in those clothes Liz Farrell makes for the dramatic society. Well, I know the Willoughbys are well off, but material possessions don't give anyone *value*, do they? As for Helen Willoughby, I've never heard such an affected voice in the whole of my life. Paula mimics her, you know, she's very cruel. And Reggie—good grief— straight out of a nineteen-thirties farce—and look what *he's* done. Not that I *know* any of them, I mean, they're not friends—but everyone knows *about* the Willoughbys— especially now.'

'So this woman started talking to Paula, did she?'

'Well, I don't know what about, I wasn't standing close, and I was busy with those people, then some friends of *theirs* came along, so we were all talking. Oh, I don't know.' Petulantly, she shrugged off the effort to remember.

'Was anyone else there? Reggie? Their friend?'

'You mean that older man. A real eye for the ladies *that* one. Well, they were round about but . . . Oh, I know—Paula and this woman moved away round the side of the stand so they could all have been there for I know. Then Paula pops her head round and says, 'Cover for me, will you, Melanie? I won't be long.' And off she went. I was furious, she's always doing things like that. And she *knew well enough* I had to get back to pick up Fiona from her ballet class—'

'Do you mean she went off with this woman?'

'Well, I don't know about *with*. I told you they'd gone round the side of the stand and I only saw Paula pop her head round—whether they both went off together—how would I know?'

'Did she say anything when she came back?'

'Came back? You don't know Paula. When she says "Cover for me," it means she's gone for good. Oh, she never came back; just when it was getting desperate Reggie and that other chap turned up, so I could get away. I never stopped to ask anything. Why should I be interested, anyway?'

'Not interested enough to say anything about this when you recognised her from the posters.'

'I *didn't*, I never claimed to *recognise* her. I just thought, later, long after the whole business, that there might be a *resemblance*. And my husband said I wasn't to—he told me—I mean, we talked it over and agreed that it's really nothing at all to do with us. We're not having the kiddies associated with murder—and suicide—If I thought Liz Farrell would go to the police, I'd never said—I *daren't* tell Trevor. You won't come back, will you? I mean, what does any of it matter now, anyway . . .' Floundering, sheep-like face suddenly twisted, Melanie said, 'Listen, just because Paula is an *acquaintance* it doesn't mean I have anything to do with her family. Let them shit on their own doorstep, they're not doing it on mine.'

*　　　*　　　*

Hunter read through the file—the report of the murder, the résumé of the crime, statements—trawling for something that might have become relevant in the light of what he had lately learned.

'It's not much,' he said to Collier. 'But it's something, it alters the perspective. You know Annette went to the Railway with Miss Farrell last Thursday. It's all right, you didn't have to

227

tell me, it was in her own time. As a matter of fact, it's surprising how well those girls have done digging up the past. Feminine intuition.' Did that sound condescending? Sexist? Could you be sexist with a homosexual? Such a thought would never have occurred to him before but he was quietly in something of a stew about this whole business. 'Did Annette tell you Liz's theory?'

'Yes.'

'Don't be so fucking neutral.'

'Sorry, guv. Annette thinks there could be something in it. I agree with her.' He could hardly say it answered all sorts of questions they hadn't even thought to ask. He had a suspicion that was exactly how Hunter felt.

'Well, if that's the case, then this man—this dangerous man from the past—has to be someone known to, close to, or connected with, the Willoughbys. The last thing he needs to know is what Liz's up to. When's Annette due back from leave?'

'Tomorrow.'

'Good. There are one or two things I need to sort out in my mind. You know that at the moment I'll involve as few people as possible in this. You don't have to agree.'

Collier looked shocked. 'Of course I will. So will Annette.'

*   *   *

228

They sat in the companionable quiet of one of Hunter's favourite Frog and Nightgown pubs. He said, 'Tell it not in Gath, publish it not in the streets of Askelon,' and took a reflective pull of his pint.

Annette sent a distress signal to Collier, who indicated similar incomprehension. They sipped their drinks and waited.

It was only fair to them that Hunter explain. 'I haven't got any fresh evidence, until I do you know I can't show my hand, make use of any official resources. So anything you do will be off the record.'

The cautionary tone made no noticeable impression on their eagerness. They had talked it over between themselves; come to the conclusion he would not put his reputation out on a limb unless he was getting close to the point where he could go to the DCS and ask for the investigation to be re-opened.

Hunter said, 'I had a chat with George Withers yesterday. He can't add anything new but he does corroborate what you and Liz learned about Beattie's mother. Object lesson. He couldn't know it was in any way relevant because it never surfaced in our enquiries. Why didn't it?'

'Because we didn't ask the right questions,' Annette said apologetically.

'Correct. We don't ask. People don't tell us things. Ergo, we can't detect a fart in a paper bag.'

229

'Did he remember anything about it?' Collier asked.

'Yes, he did, he remembers all the talk about the time it happened—it was the local sensation.'

'Had you moved away from there by then?' Annette asked.

'No, I was still there, just about. I'm buggered if I can remember a thing. Either I wasn't listening or not interested; it's just disappeared inside my memory bank. Now, I'll tell you how I think we should approach this. Until we establish where Beattie was that night between leaving the bus shelter and being seen at Miller's Bridge, we have no room to move.'

Collier looked puzzled. Hunter waited. He said hesitantly, 'Guv . . . Wouldn't it be more to the point to find out where she was going?'

'She was going to Liz's.'

Two astonished faces. The rapid progress of understanding. Collier said, 'You knew she was keeping something back. That was it.'

'Part of it.' Hunter explained, in detail but wasting no words, and—sensing for an instant some baffled hurt in Annette—emphasised, 'She genuinely didn't believe it was Beattie that Reggie was seeing at her house. She didn't come across the bracelet until the day after she'd been to the Railway with you. She came straight to me with it.'

Collier asked if it had been tested for fingerprints.

'Not yet, we'll be lucky if we can get anything off it with such small surfaces. If we do, I've no doubt they'll be Beattie's. But that isn't going to help until I've put the rest of the picture together.' He told them about his call on Melanie Beadnall. 'I wanted Paula's version of this so I went across the square straight away. It'd help to get a good look at those photos or whatever it was on the stand that took Beattie's interest. However, Mrs Pilling wasn't in. We'll go and see her in the morning, Annette, but, before that, Collier, I want you to do some checking up.'

Collier listened, nodded, unsurprised; he had been following the course of Hunter's mind.

'Now, Annette, you and I are going to call on Mrs Pilling in the morning, but before that, this is what I want you to do . . .'

This time, when he had finished, the reaction could not have been more different. Annette stared him without speaking.

'And when I say discreet, I mean as in egg-shells. Walking on.'

'I don't believe . . .' Annette began, then stopped. She saw from his face that she would have to. 'Bloody hell,' she said dazedly.

*   *   *

On the Friday evening Liz had not been home more than a few minutes before Helen rang.

231

'Darling, I know we arranged you were to come round, do you mind terribly if I put you off? I've had an invitation . . .' She mentioned friends, known slightly to Liz.

'I'm so pleased you feel like going out, of course I don't mind.' But there was something—disturbing. An edginess. 'Are you all right?'

'Why shouldn't I be?'

'Um, you seem rather . . . Helen, has anything happened?'

'What on earth are you talking about, what could have happened?'—the delicately modulated voice snapping out the words. Liz stood silent. What dreadful thing had she done to make Helen—*snap*. Then, 'Oh, I'm so sorry, Liz, I'm in rather a rush and—and—I have to admit, I have been worrying. Thinking over what we said last Saturday.'

'I really didn't mean to upset you, Helen.'

'I know you didn't. But it has rather been playing on my mind. I want the gossip to die down, I want to feel I can go about amongst people without being pointed out, whispered about.'

'I'm sure you're mistaken about that . . .' Liz could genuinely offer encouragement and sympathy, but she had to find a way to salve her conscience. She dare not say anything about sending Hunter round to see Melanie. It occurred to her that she was building up a great deal of deceit; it couldn't go on

232

indefinitely; one day she was going to have a lot of explaining to do to Helen.

The change of plan prompted Liz to phone friends in the dramatic society. It turned out there were urgent production matters to go over, which could not have been more convenient as the serious talking would be done in the local bistro and she would not have to bother making supper.

Just as she was about to go out, Wilfred telephoned. 'Look, Liz, don't say anything to Helen about this, I don't want her getting upset. She might not, but you never know.'

'What is it, Wilfred?'

'If only I knew, dear girl. I've just had a visit from one of our local CID men. Nice chap, I know him slightly, drink at the same watering holes. He was very polite, even seemed a little embarrassed.'

'About what?'

'About wanting to know where I was the night that woman drowned.'

'*What!*'

'He said it was for purposes of elimination and quite unofficial. He was just helping out the lads at Chatfield . . .'

He said more; Liz, not listening, felt blighted. When he had finished, she said in a small voice, 'Wilfred, I'm so sorry, I think this could be my fault.'

'Shopped me, have you?'

'Wilfred, don't joke. I feel awful. I'm putting

233

my foot in it all over the place.'

'Just as a matter of vulgar curiosity, what *have* you done?'

'It's too complicated to explain now. I've been finding out some things that put a different construction on what happened with Reggie and—that woman. Things to do with the past. Helen has no idea—you know how much stress she's been under, she just wants it all forgotten, everything to get back to normal.'

'You can see her point.'

'Of course I can. But on the other hand, I can't bear the thought of poor, inoffensive Reggie being blamed for something he didn't do, something so dreadful. I'm just so sorry, Wilfred, that you've become involved—I never thought for one minute . . . Er, everything's all right, isn't it?'

'You mean about my alibi? Somewhat embarrassing.'

'Oh, dear, you mean . . .'

'Yes. A lady.'

'Married?'

'Of course. Husband away on business trip.'

'What have I *done*,' Liz whispered.

'It's not the end of the world. I'm told she'll be assured of absolute discretion—as I was—so I think she'll verify what I said. If not, I'm in the soup. I can't phone her till tomorrow to find out. I would just like to know, though, Liz, what it is you've been up to.'

'Of course, I owe you an explanation. I'll write to you.'

'Write be damned. Why don't I come over and see you?'

'You know you can't, you have to see Helen and me.'

He sighed. 'But can we manage to have a private chat?'

'We'll have to, I'm getting into deep water over this. I don't think that was the right thing to say. Oh, bugger. Look, I'll speak to Helen about you coming for a visit and one of us will phone you over the weekend. And Wilfred, I really am sorry.'

CHAPTER TWENTY-ONE

Saturday morning Hunter and Annette sat in his car in Victoria Square while the rain bounced off the roof and streamed down the windows. They went over the enquiries Annette had carried out earlier that morning. She said, 'You've not heard from James yet?'

'No, shouldn't be long, though. Right, let's have a go at this one.'

They sprinted from the car, skipping over bricks in Paula's front garden and cramming themselves into the cluttered porch. They couldn't hear the bell inside the house so Hunter knocked while Annette turned back to study the Square, well-kept and pleasing even on such a day; then her gaze moved slowly over Paula's garden. 'She must drive the neighbours *insane*.'

'They get up petitions, according to Liz. Doesn't make the slightest difference, Paula has the moral superiority—it's all for good causes, the shirtless in Buenos Aires or the eyeless in Gaza or some damn thing. Bloody woman isn't in.'

'No.' They had given her long enough. They tried again, though, finding their way round the side entrance and gazing unbelievingly into the conservatory. As they retraced their steps back on to the pavement, a woman with umbrella, boots and Jack Russell terrier was emerging from the next gate. It was hardly the weather to stand about chatting but as she was obviously the no-nonsense kind who wouldn't let a little rain put her off, Hunter thought it was worth a try. 'Do you know if Mrs Pilling's away?'

'Oh, no, she went out earlier on. You called the other day, didn't you? I thought I recognised you. You're a policeman, aren't you? I saw you on TV about finding that woman's body at Miller's Bridge.' She studied Hunter with an entirely frank and unobjectionable interest.

'I don't seem to have much luck, missing Mrs Pilling again.'

'Luck hasn't a great deal to do with it. You

didn't miss her before. She was in, she just didn't open the door to you.' She said this in a matter-of-fact way, inured to Paula's eccentricities.

'Are you sure?' Hunter asked.

'Quite sure. I happened to go upstairs just after I saw you leave here—I can see all the way across the back gardens, there's an alleyway, it used to be for horses and carriages, now it's garages. I saw her go out of her back and take her car out. I assume she wanted to avoid you, not that it's any of my business, it's best to let her get on with whatever it is she's doing.' She looked eloquently at the tip that was Paula's front garden. 'One way and another, Mrs Pilling leaves much to be desired as a neighbour.'

'But she really has gone out this morning?'

'Oh, yes. Check up for yourself if you want. There's no need to go to the end of the Square and round, go along the side here. That is,' she sighed, 'if you can get through.'

They went back, past the conservatory, took a path where they were crowded to single file by dripping bushes; through a straggled place that had once been a garden. In the alleyway the buildings that had once been coach houses and stables were now garages. Paula's was empty, the doors standing open.

'Oh, well,' Hunter said. 'Let's get on.'

They sat for a while in his car, discussing strategy; it was essential Annette understand what was in his mind, so they could work step by step. As they were ready to go Hunter's mobile phone rang—the call he had been expecting from Collier. The conversation was short and unsatisfactory '. . . so we've drawn a blank on both of them. I'm desperate enough to try daft Uncle William in Cheltenham. No, only joking,' Hunter said with utmost gloom . . .

They sat silently in the car for a few moments, thinking. Hunter said, 'Robert Salter's father is clean as a whistle, not so much as a parking offence, ever, a long and blameless life. And a watertight alibi—as you know.'

'Mmm. I have to admit I took to him when I interviewed him, a sort of sparky, tough little man, really straight.'

'Liz calls him the Running Elf.'

'What?'

'It's his hobby. Athletics. Runs in over-sixties marathons.'

'*Mens sana in corpore sano . . .*'

'*Pro bono publico*, as well, I shouldn't wonder. Then there's Wilfred. I understand women find him delicious.'

Annette looked casual. Liz couldn't have told him about their girl talk at the funeral? No, she wouldn't . . .

'—hope they feel the same way about me when I'm his age. Fortunately Collier has a pal down in that part of Hampshire so he could set things going last night on an informal basis.

And with kid gloves. Because his business reputation is unspotted, likewise domestic—if priapic: retired, widower etc. And it would seem his alibi stands up for that night—

'And they're the only ones we know of in the right age range.'

'Yes.' Hunter made a sound of exasperation. 'There's something staring me in the face, I wish to Christ I knew what it was.'

*   *   *

For the second time they stood in the porch at Woodside. Annette felt tense and a little sick—which was absurd; this was just part of an on-going investigation, just like any other. Only it didn't feel like any other. She glanced sideways at Hunter; his absorbed look told her nothing. Then he turned his head, his expression changed: a communicative look, a half-smile. He nodded towards the closed door, said softly, 'I'm ready for my close-up now, Mr de Mille.'

Annette gulped, at once felt better. If only because of the reversion to the habit of wondering what the bloody hell he was saying to himself inside his head, and why. She recognised it, of course, whispered, 'Gloria Swanson. *Sunset Boulevard.*'

'Ah, I forgot you were an aficionado.'

Annette thought again. And understood why.

Helen opened the door, looked at them without speaking. She was carefully dressed and made up; her face was strange to Annette—proud and haunted. She stepped aside, invited them in with a courteous gesture, led them to the sitting room where the lowering morning had filtered in through rain-streaked glass; a shadowiness tinged with violet. It was disturbing, as disturbing as Helen's silence—a woman so schooled in social conformity, who would have at her command an entire vocabulary of automatic murmurs: *Good morning, please come in, do sit down, how may I help* . . .

But Helen said nothing; sat down, gracefully erect; the rigidity of her arms, her clasped hands, the only indication of tension. Hunter moved a chair slightly so that he could sit facing her. She regarded him with polite, if remote, interest. Annette remained standing. Mobility had its advantages.

Hunter said easily. 'Would you be good enough to help us, Miss Willoughby, by recollecting the night Beattie Booth drowned. Just a few details?' He paused. She inclined her head. 'Thank you. You and your brother went out at roughly the same time—I believe that's what you said?' He waited. Well-mannered but uncomprehending, she nodded. 'Yes. And you spent the evening with a friend —a regular Thursday evening sick visit— returning home quite late—elevenish? You'd gone to bed by the time your brother returned, roughly midnight.'

She spoke then—her sweet, precise articulation. 'I can't be sure of the exact times, but, yes, that would be approximately correct.'

'Your friend is Miss Martha Riggs, yes? She lives on the Knutsford road—those Victorian houses overlooking the Green. Pleasant backwater, that . . . It'd be about, what? Ten minutes by car, I should think . . .' He took his time, fishing out his pocket book, turning pages. 'Miss Riggs is a frail old lady, I gather, sometimes rather confused. It would be very difficult for her to recall dates and times.'

'I am sure—' Helen made a perfectly judged forward movement (in another age it would have been a bow), charmingly and earnestly teaching him manners. '—I am sure you would not be so inconsiderate as to question her.'

'Oh, good heavens, of course not, absolutely not,' Hunter agreed readily.

It was controlled, but to their experienced eyes unmistakable. The relaxation of tension —as if someone in that room had uttered the merest breath of a sigh.

'But you said . . . if I can just find it . . .' Hunter laboriously returned to his notes. The words were not written there, they were in the repository of his brain—waiting for rediscovery precisely because they told him what he needed to know. 'You said . . . ah . . . here . . . *day and night aren't always readily*

241

distinguishable to her.'

'Not unusual in the old, Mr Hunter.'

'Very true. In view of that it would be pointless to expect her to corroborate your timetable. However, I think, WPC Jones—perhaps you . . .?' He looked hopefully towards Annette, who briskly produced her pocket book.

Hunter said, 'That row of houses on The Green—villas, I think the Victorians called them—very nice . . . The one where Miss Riggs lives is converted into flats, she has a small first floor flat—well, as she doesn't get about she doesn't need anything more spacious, and she does have a lovely outlook on to The Green. There are three others, I think, larger ones . . .' He looked to Helen for confirmation; she returned a quizzical glance, as if trying to work out why he had started to ramble. '—you know the owners of those flats, and they know you. Yes. On the evening we're speaking of—' he paused.

Annette said, 'You stayed only half an hour with Miss Riggs, leaving at about 7.30.'

Helen's reaction was a small, surprised sound; she put her hand to her mouth, frowned thoughtfully. After a moment her face lightened. 'Ah, it's true there have been one or two occasions when poor Martha needed only to sleep and then there was really nothing to do except tuck her in and leave her to it. The old are never predictable, as I'm sure you'll appreciate. Yes—there could very well have been one of those occasions round about that time—not *that* evening—the neighbours obviously confused it with another occasion. After all, one would not expect them to remember with accuracy—it was just another evening to them, but in view of what transpired, it had so much more significance to me.'

Hunter, following closely, leaned forward, puzzled. 'So . . . what you are saying is that you stayed with Miss Riggs, didn't leave her till approximately quarter to eleven, and arrived home here at say, eleven.'

For the first time, Helen smiled. 'Precisely, Mr Hunter.'

A pause. A testing silence.

At last, Hunter said, 'Will you reconsider what you have just said?'

She was perfectly composed. 'I can see no reason to.'

Hunter looked down at his notebook as if uncertain. Annette said, 'Perhaps you made another call that evening after leaving Miss Riggs—went somewhere else—and have forgotten.'

'I made no more calls.'

Hunter nodded, sighed, put his pocket book away. He sat back, strong hands comfortably folded. Annette drifted, eventually settling on the arm of a well-upholstered chair, quietly engaged with her notes.

Helen, distracted, followed Annette's movements. At last, when the room seemed to have regained its equilibrium, she turned back to Hunter. He said, 'On the night when your brother failed to turn up at the bus shelter to collect Beattie, there was nothing for her to do except start walking. The next time she was seen—the last time anyone saw her alive—was shortly before nine when she approached Miller's Bridge. Now . . . what was she doing all that time? Where was she? Who was she with?'

Helen sat unmoving, her expression detached.

Hunter nodded, as if in agreement, as if she had communicated something decisive. 'Yes, of course. The important thing was to establish her *route*. She had a choice. I—er—think I've got it right, WPC Jones? Just past the end of the old Hambling Road—'

'Yes. Pinfold Lane, goes off to the left. Eventually it joins the main road about quarter of a mile before Miller's Bridge.'

'Not much used, I understand.'

'By motorists, no. It's very winding, rather a nuisance.'

As they talked, Annette occasionally consulting her notes, Helen held her poise, politely waiting for them to complete their arcane conversation and leave. As the exchange continued she was drawn irresistibly to follow it, shifting her position, turning her

244

head.

'But then, of course, Beattie was walking.'

'Yes, guv, she'd never had a car.'

'No . . . She was used to finding her way about, the distance wasn't too great, she was dressed for the rain. And Pinfold Lane is the shorter route.'

'So, logically, we'd expect her to take it. Wouldn't you agree, Miss Willoughby?' Hunter asked.

'I really can't see my agreement would affect the course of this conversation,' Helen said levelly.

'Oh, wouldn't you?' Hunter enquired pleasantly. 'Well, as you're local, and you know the lie of the land, so to speak, you would know that the shortest way from the bus shelter to Liz's would be by Pinfold Lane.'

Helen said nothing, her face was expressionless.

Annette came to stand by her chair. 'You knew, of course, that Reggie was in the habit of taking Beattie to Liz's?'

Helen cast about, trying to get her mental balance.

'Liz would have told you,' Hunter said, matter-of-fact. 'She wouldn't, of course, have told anyone else, but as you're both so close—

Helen said, 'She told *you*?'

'Ah, it's our business to know all sorts of things.'

Annette hovered, solicitous. 'You did *know,*

245

didn't you—I mean about Reggie using Liz's house as a kind of lark—so like him. How long have you known, Miss Willoughby?'

'I didn't say I—

Hunter said, 'Oh, you mean it wasn't Liz who told you? It was someone else?'

'No. That is—

Hunter said to Annette, 'Can you think of anyone else who knows?'

'Unless Liz told someone as well as you, Miss Willoughby. Did she say she had?'

'She would say nothing of the sort—'

'No, I agree, it wouldn't be likely . . . You didn't mention it to anyone? After Liz told you?'

'This is absurd—'

'Yes, it is really, just not the kind of thing you'd chat casually about—'

'I have *never*—Oh, this is so confusing, so—' Helen tilted her head down, put her fine-bred hand to her brow.

Hunter rose from his chair. 'I'm sorry, are you feeling faint? Would you like WPC Jones to fetch you a glass of water?'

'No, I would not,' Helen said shortly, looking for an instant as if she was about to pick up the nearest delicate china ornament and hurl it at Hunter. She made an effort at composure, unnecessarily patting her hair into place. Her fingers trembled.

The merest hint of a nod from Hunter to Annette . . .

246

Earlier, talking it over, he told her what he knew—'But then there's all the rest I *don't* know. I have to get her to tell me . . .'

He had been working towards it, using anything, whatever opportunity offered, seeking the hairline crack in Helen's defence.

'Of course,' Hunter said, hand to forehead, triumphantly making a discovery, turning to Annette. 'When we were talking about her route—Now, how's this? Instead of turning left, if she'd kept straight on, she'd be on the main road. Straight to Miller's Bridge, then on to Liz's.'

'Yes, and she'd know it because that's the way Reggie would have driven her.'

'Exactly.' He pondered. 'And . . . Just a short stretch of it is along Woodside. Right past here, as a matter of fact.'

They were both silent, standing looking down at Helen. When she did not speak, Hunter said quietly, 'Isn't that so, Miss Willoughby?'

'I really can't think what all this . . . I don't know what you're . . .'

Hunter resumed his seat. His voice was kind and calm. 'Beattie told you, didn't she? She was looking for Reggie—she knew this was his home, he'd pointed it out to her once when they drove past. She was very angry, she suspected he had stood her up—and she was right. Just after you arrived back here from your shortened visit to—'

'I stayed with Martha, I stayed with her the usual time,' Helen said in a voice that was toneless, from which the strength had gone.

'You left her early. You came back here. And Beattie knocked on the door. Didn't she?' He waited.

She looked away from him, gazing towards the window with eyes that saw nothing.

Hunter spoke quietly, without accusation. 'When I asked myself where Beattie was that missing hour and a half, I knew there was only one place where she logically could be. Here . . . But in that weather she'd hardly be waiting outside. She'd keep going, on to Liz's—delayed, yes—in the hope of finding Reggie there. Because he wasn't *here,* his alibi held. So did yours . . . Until I looked at it more closely and realised it was worthless. That old lady couldn't remember what had happened five minutes before, much less testify to your presence. Who could? The neighbours. They knew you, your footsteps, your car . . . And when we discovered from them that you had lied to us about the time you left . . . We knew you would have only one reason.'

He was silent, watching her. Eventually, she said, 'You are not going to believe me if I deny it.'

'You aren't going to deny it because it's true. And it's time you told the truth about this, isn't it?'

She crossed her arms, hugging herself; she
248

had grown very pale. Annette took a seat beside her. 'Are you cold? Would you like me to get you a cardigan?'

'If you'd be kind enough to switch on the fire—it's quite a simple mechanism. I was in the kitchen when you called, it's warm there . . . Thank you.' She sat ordering her thoughts. 'I've never done anything wrong in my life before this. The burden of guilt has been almost more than I can bear. At times, I just wanted to . . . Yes. She came here. You know why, don't you? Oh, she was looking for Reggie—but do you know why? Why . . . all of it.'

'Her mother. All those years ago.' Hunter had not the faintest idea which direction to move after that, there was no solid ground beneath his feet; but he sat looking as authoritative as if his entire consciousness was inscribed with every last particle of the doings of the Willoughby family.

'All those years ago, indeed,' Helen murmured. 'How did you . . . No matter, that's your job, isn't it? To find out secrets. And I think, without any idea of what she was doing, my dear Liz—' Pain crossed her face, at once shut away behind a calm pride. 'I opened the door and that woman pushed past me, shouting, "Where is he?" and swearing, going in and out of the rooms, shouting and swearing. If anyone had been here . . . I thought perhaps I should call the police—but she kept shouting Reggie's name, and it's my instinct to protect him. I began to understand what she was saying. That she and Reggie had been—that he was now trying to avoid her—she was not going to be cast aside—I managed to calm her somewhat, although that scarcely helped, her rage simply became more focussed. This woman I had never set eyes on in my life had a very special hatred for me. I was attempting to influence Reggie, to "come between them". She called me the most insulting names . . .' She lost momentum, perhaps in the recollection of shock, sat looking helplessly down at her hands.

By the subtlest of indications, Hunter passed to Annette: *this is woman's work.*

Annette said, 'Until that moment, Miss Willoughby, you really had no idea he had formed this relationship? Look, what I'm trying to say—when my brother's involved with someone, his manner changes, little things . . . I can't say I *know*, but some sixth sense tells me what's going on.'

'How understanding you are. Now I can see why Liz likes you so much.'

Oh, Christ, I haven't *got* a brother . . . Hunter's eye upon her, professional, approving: *you'll do well.*

'Of course I knew there was something. But, you must understand . . . Reggie did have—flirtations, but always such nice girls. I would have thought she was making it all up, but, no,

250

she *knew* Reggie. It was she who told me they used Liz's house—they had to be secret, until they were ready to approach me. Only . . . time was going by, she had become impatient, and it was only too evident Reggie had changed his mind about their—about—He was supposed to marry her—' She spoke not in rejection but incredulity; however often she might replay the scene in her mind she had never managed to make herself believe in anything so preposterous. 'It was something she regarded as owing to her. If he refused, if I attempted to put obstacles in their way, she would make scenes all over Hambling, she would let everyone know what had been going on, and why. I tried to reason with her, I tried to bribe her. She didn't want money, not of itself, she wanted status, security, respect. She wanted first place here, as Reggie's—wife. It was unthinkable. I would be allowed to stay, provided I behaved; if not, she told me in the plainest, coarsest terms, that she would make my life hell.'

'Surely,' Annette said, 'you didn't believe he would agree to anything like that?'

'No, that was why I tried to calm her, to find out how this—this nightmare had come about. It soon became obvious that he hadn't known what she had in mind when they began this—association. When he realised that everything was getting completely out of hand—he tried to buy her off. But no . . .'

'We began to suspect, early in our enquiries, that Beattie was putting pressure on him,' Hunter lied comfortably. 'She was a tough woman, she'd had a hard life, he'd have a devil of a job standing up to her. And he felt sorry for her—after all, she did have a grievance.'

'Of course she had a grievance. Unfortunately, she had made him the means of settling it. I would have been only too relieved to compensate her in other ways. It was my duty, after all.'

Hunter took out his handkerchief, coughed politely into it. It was a sign that he had no idea what Helen was talking about. Annette signalled back in silent panic: *neither do I.* Time to tread softly.

'Yes, yes, I can see that,' Hunter said judicially. 'This was all the heat of the moment—fury for her, distress for you. Didn't you think that given time, a little calming down—'

'I didn't *think* at all, Mr Hunter. That woman and I didn't speak the same language. She had made up her mind that the price of her recompense was marriage to Reggie. Her entitlement, she called it. She was frightening and threatening and she had every intention of shattering my life, and Reggie's and Liz's. She went out as she had come, yelling and violent. She was going to Liz's—she had got it into her head that Reggie would eventually turn up there. She intended to stay until he did, even if

252

it took days—she had nothing else to do. And she would make herself known to the neighbours—unless he put in an appearance. Then she stamped off, down the drive, out of the gate. I stood there, in the hall, watching her. I couldn't move. My mind had seized up. I don't know how long it was before . . .' She shook her head, bewildered.

'What did you do?' Hunter asked softly.

'It's odd. I don't remember. Oh, I know what I did but I simply don't remember *doing* it. I put on my coat, got my car out . . . and went after her.'

CHAPTER TWENTY-TWO

The sky was so dark Liz had to turn the lights on in her house. The rain was all around, beating, gushing, drumming, the noise so invasive she hesitated once, up in her workroom, wondering if she had imagined the sound of someone trying the kitchen door. A few moments later the front doorbell rang and she went to answer it. A figure stood in the porch against the deluged background—a figure so shrouded in rainwear that for a mad instant she thought it was old Mr Truelove. What was he doing on her doorstep?

Then she recognised Paula, groaned inwardly recalling their last meeting. Paula

253

thrust past her, marched into the kitchen, where she stood dripping, removing her sou'wester. Her expression was so unpleasant Liz came to a full stop in the kitchen doorway. *Oh, God, not another scene.*

Paula's voice was flat and harsh. 'You ignored me. You ignored what I said to you.' Released from the sou'wester, her beautiful hair slid and rippled round her shoulders. Her face was blotchy; she always had a staring look, now her eyes seemed fixed.

Liz suppressed a rush of irritation, leaned against the doorjamb, arms folded, the picture of relaxation. 'Good morning, Liz, may I come in? Please do, how are you, Paula? Fine, and you?—'

'Shut up, you supercilious bitch. Why can't you mind your own business? Do you know who phoned me the other night? That fucking stupid Melanie Beadnall. Screeching at me from the minute I picked up the phone—"Tell that bitch Liz Farrell to stop sending the police here—" I never spoke, not a word—just hung up when she'd finished. *And* that sanctimonious old bag who lives next door to me took great pleasure in telling me a policeman had called on Thursday. As if I didn't know, I saw him cross the square from Melanie's so I didn't answer the door. I've got nothing to say to him and I'm damned if I want to listen to him.'

Not speaking on the phone, not answering

the door . . . Perhaps some awful illness had come upon Paula, making her reclusive, paranoid. Liz moved forward, steadying hand outstretched, 'Paula, are you all right?'

Paula knocked her hand away with bruising force. 'Keep your concern for yourself, you're going to need it. You sent him round there, didn't you? Didn't you?'

'Well, yes, all right. I did. But just calm down and listen. I tried to get hold of you first, when Melanie told me, last Sunday. To talk to you—after all, it sounded so odd she could have got it wrong. And then, when I couldn't get in touch with you, in the week, I thought I'd speak to DCI Hunter—'

'Oh, yes,' Paula sneered. 'This is the general run of police work, is it? He harasses and badgers inoffensive members of the public as a favour to you so he can get inside your knickers.'

'Just which inoffensive members of the public did you have in mind? Melanie? A minute ago you were calling her a fucking bitch. You? As you made sure you weren't available I don't see what you've got to complain about.'

'Oh, don't you? Then I'll tell you. I'm complaining about you poking about where you've no right to be. You think you're going to drag me in and ruin everything now—well, you're wrong, Miss Spiffing Clever Private Eye. Got that?'

'No, Paula, I haven't. I don't know what you're talking about and—'

'Oh, *really. Well* . . . Didn't you *detect* it— even with sheep-face Melanie's help? No? You couldn't smell shit if you stuck your nose in it—

They'd had their bad times, they'd had their quarrels, but never had Liz felt the onslaught of so much hatred. Behind Paula's fidgeting and sneering and mockery there was a disturbing recoil of hysteria. This could be some imagined, invented wrong. Liz tried to work out what it could be.

She had sent Hunter to Melanie . . . It seemed that all that had achieved was confusion and Paula's rage. One last try— 'Look, can we talk this over—'

'There's no talking, there's no talking. You're going to do as I say, that's all.'

'In that case, Paula, bugger off out of here—' Something like a mental snag, catching on delayed bewilderment. 'What did you mean? Drag you in? Ruin everything?' But as she asked, she knew. She knew by the smugness on Paula's face, she knew by hints and ambiguities and half-recognised thoughts. Everything coalesced into a moment of understanding that had been waiting, waiting, for her to come upon it.

'It was you, you who found Beattie, and arranged for her and Reggie to meet . . .'

'Uh . . . uh . . . uh . . .' Paula mimed a

moronic inarticulateness. 'You're as dim as she was.'

'How could you do it to him!' Liz shouted. 'How could you involve him with something so—'

'So sordid? Life is. Life is dirty secrets from the past and Reggie falling for any heart-rending story anyone tells him; Reggie playing the knight errant and thinking it's such a lark, bringing her here in secret—until the stupid cow started wanting things her way, trying to take over. She was so ignorant she could scarcely even read, but she thought *she* could tell *me* what to do.'

Liz had the surreal experience of hearing her own painstakingly constructed theory verified by Paula's quarrel with herself—details, arrangements, added. Paula pacing angrily, '. . . nobody had ever treated her decently before—stupid old bag couldn't recognise it for what it was—decided he'd *fallen* for her—making herself *glamorous* for him . . . I told her she'd frighten him off—'

Liz cried, 'I just don't know how he could be involved in *anything* with you.'

'You still haven't got it, have you?' Paula stopped pacing, looked at her contemptuously. '*He didn't know.* That I was pulling Beattie's strings. He thought she'd managed to find out on her own, working things out. He thought she was "splendid" for all her disadvantages to track him down as the only one able to help

257

her. Good God, d'you think I'd be stupid enough to let him know I started it—he'd get cold feet, he always did, always went running to Helen; he'd have spilled the whole lot when he was questioned if he'd thought I'd bail him out.' Paula began to range backwards and forwards again, limbs unco-ordinated; she collided with a cupboard, shook herself angrily, then obviously losing track, shouted, 'It would have worked—she ruined it—' A thought stopped her; her look, furtive, turned away.

'Everything was ruined for her,' Liz said harshly. 'You brought about her death.'

Paula shrugged. 'Woman like that, bound to come to grief, runs in the family. The police weren't all that bothered, were they? Went through the motions, then just dropped it. Then—then *you* started . . . Do you know how dangerous you are?'

*   *   *

I went after her . . .

But this time Hunter and Annette accompanied her as she drove through the black, pelting night with no thought of anything but another desperate appeal, no recollection of seeing anyone until the bright lights of Miller's Bridge. Almost like a stage set: the lonely figure glancing back, moving closer to the parapet to let the motorist past, then turning, standing transfixed . . .

Because Helen had stopped, then let the car creep forward. And Beattie, with her street survival reflexes, knew that Helen had followed her, that Helen had been pushed too far, become dangerous.

Seeing the woman with the power to do so much harm, who had abused and tormented her, terrified into stillness, brought out in Helen a rush of wildness she had never known in her life. Now she was the one with the power, and there was a hell-bent atavism in turning from prey to hunter.

She shot forward a few feet, stopped with a screech of brakes. Beattie began to move, edging crabwise, scrambling, pressing herself against the stonework. Helen raced the engine, crashed the gears, reversed, drove forward again to within inches of Beattie, playing the dreadful game of *pretending* to run into her. Unable to stop herself, unable to say, ever, if she could really have done it.

The decision was not hers. Beattie somehow got on to the parapet and then, straddling, crawling, casting one fearful look back, lost balance, threw out her arms in a toppling gesture, and was gone.

There was only the sound of rain, the rushing water. The stage was empty, the drama had concluded—with nothing to show it had taken place. Except Beattie's handbag lying in the road, lying there in the garish persistence of its size and cheapness, blazoning the reality of the woman, the presence of the woman in that place.

Helen drove forward, opened the car door, scooped it up. Drove on, reversed, went home.

By the time Reggie came home she was lying, fully dressed on her bed, shivering in the dark; the handbag—thrust into a supermarket carrier—pushed in the bottom of her wardrobe.

She stayed awake all night, haunted by the unreality of what had happened, what she had done, what its aftermath could be. Had Beattie survived? Could she swim? As far as Helen could reconstruct it, she had fallen very close to the outer side of the bridge, where jutting stonework was a hazard . . . Had she smashed against it, been unconscious as she hit the water? Or with the endurance of her kind had she saved herself—to find her way back, a greater threat than ever. For hours Helen stood at her bedroom window, staring down into the driveway, straining to make out in the dark the limping, lurching progress of one who had crawled from the river.

By dawn she had decided what she must do. She would never tell Reggie that Beattie had been here. She would behave in all ways as if nothing in the rhythm of their days had faltered, nothing been threatened. If Reggie had the least inkling she knew anything of what had been happening, he would break down completely. By maintaining the fiction of their unaltered days, she would sustain them both. She had the strength.

And this was what she did, waiting upon events; dissembling, managing, arranging. Her nerve was strong, her desire to protect Reggie, to preserve herself and their life together, overrode every moral consideration.

She recounted all this in a steady voice, with a restraint that spoke of profound self-knowledge. Her confession over she sat exhausted. Shriven.

Hunter went to make tea; as he left the room he looked back at Annette: *we still don't know.*

Annette knew better than to speak—except to say something mundane. 'I hate to think of my boss finding his way round your kitchen. He'll probably bring all the wrong cups.' She took Helen's hand. Helen clung to the lifeline, after a while drew back, produced her handkerchief; the suggestion of tears there and gone. 'Thank you.'

'It *is* better this way.'

'Yes, you're quite right. The guilt would have made me mad, I think, or ill. That's one obstacle overcome, a relief to the spirit.'

Hunter came in, carefully carrying a tray on which were a homely brown teapot, a carton of milk, three odd mugs and a spoon. Annette looked at it helplessly. 'Would you prefer lemon?'

'No, thank you. I must get used to doing without refinements, mustn't I? This is very welcome, thank you.'

Hunter sat down. 'Her handbag. Where is it?'

'Oh, goodness, I couldn't keep it.' She could not bear to think of it being in the house—staking some claim. She could never bring herself to look inside it, to handle the dead woman's personal effects; but she was desperate to find a way to dispose of it. At the time, there was a great deal of publicity about its whereabout, a search in progress for it; even if she could have cut it into pieces, she was terrified the pieces would be discovered if she took them to the tip, or tried to get rid of them in a waste bin somewhere. There were no fires in the house where she could burn it. Eventually, in great furtiveness, she did burn it—in the garden—locking the side entrance to the house to safeguard against interruption. Only to have Liz burst upon her from the back.

Hunter listened, looking comfortable, drinking his tea. Helen could not know how carefully he was going over every word she had said, how closely he watched her when he spoke, his scrupulously chosen questions as casually placed as if they were following a conversation that had already absorbed them.

And how long have you known about Beattie's background?'

'Oh, years . . .'

Years . . .

'. . . of course, I knew nothing of *her,* only that the woman had a daughter. How cruelly ironic. He never knew whether her mother was alive or dead when he left her . . . And I drove away from Miller's Bridge not knowing . . . I must have inherited that special kind of wickedness from him.'

Hunter, impassive beneath an avalanche of comprehension. *Of course, it had to be. Who else?*

He glanced at Annette, who hadn't picked it up. A moment later, a swiftly suppressed reaction indicated she had.

'He was a very cruel man—never physically, with us, his family—just cruel in every other possible way. He made life wretched for everyone around him. But no one had the least idea of his other self—the man who found his satisfaction in the poverty and helplessness of young prostitutes. It went on for a long time, even when Mother was alive. In his last illness he told me all about it—about the excitement he had derived from a double life of such contrast; the comfort and respectability of life here; then the streets, the slums, the dirty rooms, the sluttish women. He went into great detail, what he did to them, his enjoyment in their degradation. His language was explicit and obscene. He told me about this young woman who had been foolish enough to make demands on him, and persist in them. He told

263

me how he had beaten her, with his fists, on and on. Then he left her, in that poor house, for her child to find. Sometimes he became confused . . . once, once, he started talking to Paula about it. Fortunately, she was so taken with her own concerns she never listened—so I thought. But after he did that, I could never let him see anyone for fear of what he might say. He had never, after the event, put himself at risk by attempting to find out if he had killed the young woman. I said to you he was never physically cruel—until that act. I think the savagery of a lifetime went into that because he said—he said it satisfied him. After it he gave up his double life completely, he no longer needed it. He seemed to regard this as in some way commendable.' She paused.

Annette gave her a moment, asked, 'Did he ever name her? His victim.'

'No. He used filthy expressions, I told you he was explicit, but those women were not individuals to him, they were merely vehicles for his twisted needs. Of course, I was horrified. I thought of the utter shame if it ever became known, our family would never recover from such a scandal. My father, being what he was—put the burden of his crime on my conscience, deliberately, thinking I would be haunted by *his* guilt, by the dread of discovery, that I would know no peace for the rest of my days. But he was wrong. Quite wrong. After his death, I realised there was nothing I could do, it had all happened over twenty-five years before. I had no way of finding the woman—if she was still alive—I could make no restitution. I did the sensible thing, I put it from my mind. I really did forget it.'

Hunter said, 'It wasn't your guilt, it could have stayed forgotten. If only Beattie hadn't had a moment of idle curiosity and looked at the display on the stand at the exhibition, and seen a photograph of your father.'

'Paula meddles, she makes mischief. This was to be her *coup de grâce.* Chance put that woman her way. She saw she could use her to cause both Reggie and myself embarrassment, hurt, the anguish of living with a shameful secret, the fear of its being found out. By planting that woman in our midst, what she was and what she knew, she could guarantee to make our lives wretched.'

Annette said, 'Jealousy?'

'Such a destructive emotion. She was fostered when she was little more than a baby, she's resented it all her life, being pushed out—she always saw it as *my* doing—I had no idea it had become a rage with her to get her own back. She to make Beattie her creature— with no thought where it might lead. A woman like that—such a pathetically dull, deprived existence—to offer her the chance to right an old wrong, a glimpse of another life, secret meetings with an attractive man—it simply didn't occur to her that Beattie was living in the middle of a drama and would soon begin writing her own part. She was an ignorant woman, but she had a native cunning—even when she was here, scarcely controlled in her rage and insults—she never so much as mentioned Paula's name. She wasn't going to give away her trump card for fear, I suppose, that I might find some way of bringing Paula back into line.'

Hunter asked, 'How did you know, then, about Paula's involvement, and when did you discover it?'

'I didn't discover it, Mr Hunter, she came and told me. Yesterday.'

'Why?'

'Because, like you, she had worked it out. After all, she had engineered their meetings—Thursday, the bus shelter, seven o'clock. Knowing that, she knew that there was only one place Beattie could be that night. It was Paula's triumph, coming here yesterday, she had me exactly where she wanted me—at her mercy. She's desperate for money, her business has failed, she's taken out a second mortgage on her house. I suppose I should have read the signs—over the past year I've lent her money, Reggie did, too, but her demands became too much. I told her she must make some effort to arrange her affairs, then we'd think again. I told Reggie he must stop funding her. But now, by what she had brought about—everything was within her grasp. And that was what she demanded—everything.' Expressively, a gesture encompassed the room, the house: every furnishing, every ornament, every painting and piece of china; the garden, the cars, the investments, the ease, the elegance—even the memories of the house would pass into Paula's keeping, to do with as she wished. 'And she was prepared to blackmail me in order to get it. I would be in her power, always, and she would take everything from me, from Liz.' She paused, considering. 'When I opened the door to you I knew I had lost. But then, so has Paula.'

Hunter said, 'You'll have to come to the police station so we can talk to you about this in a formal manner. In the light of our investigations and what you've just said to me, I must tell you I am arresting you on suspicion of the murder of Beattie Booth. You're not obliged to say anything unless you wish to do so, but what you say may be put into writing and given in evidence.'

Helen nodded. 'I understand.' Then she stood up urgently, with none of her customary grace. 'Excuse me—I—'

Annette followed her in a rush from the room, into the downstairs cloakroom, stood outside the lavatory door listening to the sound of vomiting. Eventually, Helen emerged, chalk-white, to tidy herself at the wash-basin. 'I apologise. I'm all right now.'

'It's reaction.' Annette took her back to the sitting room. 'Just sit down quietly for a minute.' She busied herself soothingly, turned off the gas fire, went to pick up the tray. This gave her a view through the side window. What she saw made her turn sharply, head tilted to Hunter. He moved next to her, saw the farther side of the house, set back, that had not been visible to them at the front door.

'Miss Willoughby, where is your sister Paula?'

Helen, head back against the chair, eyes closed, said wearily, 'I have no idea.'

Hunter said, 'Her car is parked at the side.'

She was vague. 'Yes, she left it . . .'

'She's left it here since yesterday?' Annette queried. 'Since she came to see you yesterday.'

'Oh, she came again this morning. To gloat. Surprisingly briefly. Then she went off . . . to do something.'

Hunter said, 'Without her car? In this weather?'

'It's beyond me to fathom her vagaries. The rain wouldn't get to her, she was so muffled up in waterproofs—'

Hunter interrupted her. 'Where was she going? What was she going to do? Think, please, it could be important.'

Aware of urgency, Helen collected herself. 'She said she had something to attend to—no, somebody to attend to. I'm sorry, I —'

Into Hunter's mind, an unreeling of alarm:

268

Liz's enquiries—rain—waterproofs—someone on foot—He spoke rapidly to Annette, 'I'm going to Liz's. You arrange transport from Chatfield, get Miss Willoughby over there and booked in. *Before that*—get hold of Hambling—tell them I want some back-up, a couple of local lads at 42 The Bellfield. Fast as they can, tell them I'll meet them there—*silent approach*. That's vital. Got it? Do it. *Now . . .*'

CHAPTER TWENTY-THREE

'Dangerous?' Liz repeated. 'To you? Well, I'll tell you this, Paula, you're dead right. I am. I'm not going to let you get away with your part in this. I don't care about compassion and forgiveness and family feeling—I care that you've cost that woman her life, and brought about Reggie's death, and caused Helen so much suffering I don't know how she's stayed sane.'

'Helen,' Paula mimicked. 'Oh, Helen's going to thank you.'

'What do you mean?' Liz asked, suddenly uncertain.

'I mean Helen and I have come to an arrangement and there's no room for you in it anywhere.'

As she spoke, Paula looked round the kitchen carefully, assessingly, nodding to herself. Then she did something unaccountable: she went to the kitchen door, briskly unclicked the latch. While she did this she talked in such a way as if something had been agreed between them. 'No, I don't want to leave the way I came in, the front *was* a bit risky.'

Liz said, puzzled, 'Was it you—trying the back door?'

'Of course. That's how I came, along the side here—I didn't even need to walk down Bellfield.' She was staring at Liz with a superior, anticipatory smile, inviting her to understand.

It came to Liz in slow-motion—a sense of the inevitability of Paula's actions—not random, not inconsequential. This was what Paula knew she could do and get away with, because she'd done it before . . .

Liz heard the rain, looked at the muffling waterproofs, thought of the network of paths and tracks. Of silent footsteps.

'You. You went to Woodside that morning. Didn't you? You said Reggie had changed his mind, asked you not to go—but he hadn't, he waited for you at Woodside, just as you'd arranged, let you in, someone he trusted . . .' It was the look on Paula's face, the pleasure in her own cleverness, that made Liz master her growing anger. She needed to know the truth and what she had to do to get it was pretend to be overawed—Paula would have no trouble believing that: admiration was her due.

270

She made her voice falter, 'And you dictated that note, but—how could you get him to . . .'

'Of course I went to Woodside. By the back way, Liz, by the back way,' she repeated softly. 'I told him there was something important he had to know, so we sat down together to talk, and because it was a nasty cold morning, we had a drink together. Only I didn't drink mine, I kept adding it to his when he wasn't looking. I told him I'd come into possession of information about Beattie's death that would clear him completely—oh, it really didn't matter what I said—he believed anything, he was so stupefied with his tranquillisers. We had another drink—*he* had another drink. I told him it was time he had some more pills; it wasn't—he had no idea what he was doing by then, just did whatever I said. He always did what anyone said, didn't he? I looked at him, so futile, so worthless—what had he ever done to deserve . . . he and Helen . . .' She lost track; paused, began again. 'I told him I had to take him somewhere where there was evidence, and we'd be late back, so he'd better leave a note for Helen. He didn't know what he wrote, just copied down as I spoke. I almost had to carry him to his car, he passed out as I put him in the driver's seat. It was easy, he didn't suffer.'

She was too absorbed in herself to care, to even notice the effect this was having on Liz. And Liz, sickened, listened to how Paula walked back home the way she had come and

271

at the right time got out her car and drove to Woodside where she parked in a lay-by in sight of number 18. 'I knew what time Helen was due back. I had to be there, she wasn't going to make that discovery alone—' Any possibility that this demonstrated humanity in Paula disappeared instantly. 'I had to make sure that note survived. Devastated Helen might be, but she wouldn't have the family name besmirched by suicide if she could help it. No, she'd have destroyed it, tried to make out it was an accident . . . If he took the blame, if he *appeared* to take the blame for the murder, then the whole thing could be wrapped up and put away. Which is exactly what happened. I was in the clear and ready for the next move. Only you . . . You started *meddling.*'

Her eyes came into focus; disturbingly, her face had an untenanted look; for Liz there was the suddenly stomach lurching suspicion that Paula might have lost her hold on reality. But it was only too easy to plead madness—all that conniving and destructiveness, it took clarity, a sense of purpose to do what Paula had done. 'You sicken and disgust me—'

Paula's eyebrows went up, interested. Conversationally, she asked, 'Don't I frighten you as well? I should, you know.' Then in a thought-out, controlled movement, she reached to her right and took the largest knife from the wall fitting of three.

A speechless moment of absolute

272

incredulity, then the fear running through her to her bones. Paula stood between her and the back door; instinctively Liz began to back away to the dining room—*what shall I do? what shall I do?* Her voice was unsteady. 'Paula, you don't mean this—'

'Oh, don't I just. In case it hasn't sunk in yet—I'm going to get rid of you, you know too much, you've got a big mouth, and you're in my way.'

Paula walked forward, the knife held before her, angled for an upward thrust. She did not seem to be in any hurry. 'No one saw me arrive, no one will see me leave. This will be an unexplained tragedy. I shall walk back to Woodside, get rid of these clothes—'

'Woodside!' Liz cried. 'What have you done to Helen?'

'Oh, darling Helen's all right. I couldn't possibly harm darling Helen, could I? Helen's going to hand over everything to me. The share I *never* had and was entitled to; Reggie's share, yours, *everything* of hers—' Her hand moved, the blade was very large, a wicked gleam in the dullness of the overcast day.

In spite of its threat, a distant anger stirred in Liz, expressed in scorn. 'Good God, Paula, why on earth should Helen pass over a farthing to you?'

'Because she killed Beattie Booth ...'

'*What!*'

273

'. . . and I'm going to see she pays for it for the rest of her life.'

A moment. She found her voice, 'Don't be so—'

'Yes, she did,' Paula shouted. '*I* worked it out, *I* did. Not you. Not the police. And you aren't going to tell them, you're not going to have the chance—'

The utter impossibility of it; the numbing sense that it could be true, came down like barriers in Liz's mind before a rush of anger. She was in danger, but that took second place to rage. She wasn't going to be menaced and attacked by this hateful woman, she wasn't going to plead for her life, she was going to be cunning, she was going to get the better of Paula and save herself . . . There was nothing coherent in this thought process; just the instinct to survive that registered every object around her and expressed itself in a play-acting faintness.

The Victorian mahogany chair. She put her hand on to its back as if to support herself, 'I just can't believe—' she had to struggle with her fury to make her voice low. Watched Paula advance—her blotchy face now livid with triumph—waited for her to get within range.

Then her hand closed on the chair back, her body swung round as a counterweight for maximum impact, and the chair smashed into Paula's body. Paula went sprawling, Liz so blindly furious she hoped she'd broken all her ribs; the action also had a vicious efficiency—as Paula reeled, her arm flung out, the knife arched, flashing, across the room—landing, thudding, Liz diving for it, grabbing it as it bounced.

As she was getting to her feet, Paula staggered upright (she was indestructible, it was those layers of clothes); Liz circled, brandishing the knife, shouting, 'I'll kill you for what you've done—' Her back was now to the kitchen door—a half formed idea of making a dash for it collided with the sound of voices, the disturbed air of other presences. Paula, looking beyond her, was screaming, 'She's mad, she's got a knife—they were in it together—her and Helen—'

From behind Liz, an arm firmly round her waist, clamping her to a solid body, a hand reaching to grasp her upraised hand, 'All right, girl, give me that,' Hunter said.

There were two uniformed policemen as well as Hunter in her house, all three necessary to hold her and Paula apart as they screamed at each other, at Hunter.

Liz: 'I *told* you, I told you. Look at her—all that—camouflage. That's how she went round to Reggie that morning—she's admitted it. She's proud of it. She's come round here—just the same—to *kill me*—'

Paula: 'She hit me with a chair. That chair—*hit me with it*. Then she came at me with that *knife*, her own knife—look from here. It's *her knife—*'

'*Liar*—she had to make sure I wouldn't tell—listen,' embarking on a high-speed, incoherent version of what Paula had told her. It made sense to her, it was simply the logical conclusion of everything they had considered. Paula began to struggle out of the grip of the policeman patiently holding her, outshouting Liz, 'This man is sexually interfering with me—'

'Oh, Christ, you and your bloody family' Hunter breathed. He raised his voice. 'Shut up,' establishing some kind of order, knowing Liz now amenable and shoving her firmly aside. 'Shut up and listen. Paula Pilling, I am arresting you for aiding and abetting the suicide of Reginald Thomas Willoughby, you do not have to say—'

Paula began to shriek, insults, obscenities, accusations. Hunter persisted, completed his caution. 'Oh, God, take her away. Take her to Chatfield.'

They must have heard her all down quiet Bellfield, struggling and shouting as she was hauled down the drive, to the road, into the police car. Rain or no rain, the neighbours would have to come out to see what was happening. Liz had temporarily stopped knowing, seeing, or caring about anything.

Hunter held her close against him; she put her head on his shoulder. He stroked her hair, murmured something inconsequential. At last she had control—of a sort. He said, 'Sit down, girl.'

She sat down, listened as he told her. Did she listen? He said, 'I have to tell you, Liz, and you must take it in. I know what Helen did, all of it. I've just come from Woodside—'

'I must go to her—' Useless decision, her limbs refused to obey.

'No, stay here, please. She confessed to the murder of Beattie Booth. She needed very much to clear her conscience.'

Liz stared at him bleakly.

'She's very composed, very dignified, as you'd expect. And much too proud to tell me her greatest concern is for you, for your love. She's afraid you'll—'

'Where is she?'

'Annette's taken her to Chatfield.'

'Under arrest.'

'Yes.'

'Please let me see her, please.'

'Of course. Before you do, you'll have to make a statement. I'll drive you to Chatfield now. You can see Annette, she'll—'

'Statement? What about?'

'Everything, Liz. Everything.'

*   *   *

Everything meant a great deal and a long time; drinking plastic cups of awful tea, she grew irritable, tearful. 'I was such a *fool*—it never occurred to me why *Paula* was so self-effacing.

277

Paula—not taking centre stage. It was because she daren't put herself in the way of having her involvement discovered. She used *me* and, oh, God, Annette, I fell for it—'

Annette, acting as shock-absorber, down-to-earth, sympathetic but brisk: *Liz, that's only your interpretation* . . . One of how many brushed aside warnings.

. . . 'you won't believe what started her off. Wilfred, of all things. That summer he spent with us. She'd got it into her head that he was going to marry Helen, that all the money, the property, would be combined with his, that if that happened she would never have a chance of getting her hands on what she thinks is hers anyway. But . . . it was all in her head . . . Wilfred marrying Helen . . . oh, hell, you can't know how ironic that is, I'll tell you one day. But by the time it had become obvious she was wrong, she'd started the whole thing rolling. It was out of control. Beattie was out of control. Then Beattie was dead—and that was driving Paula mad. When a woman's body was found, Paula knew the description was Beattie's—but she didn't know it *was* her, or what could have happened. So she made that anonymous phone call.'

'It was Paula? Liz, I've explained to you what hearsay is, you can't—'

'She *told* me. And she told me why she did it. If she landed him right in it, she'd find out through him what was going on—if the dead

278

woman *was* Beattie. But as you didn't know yourself then, and Reggie had cleared off, anyway, she had to find someone else, use someone else so she could keep herself informed, keep herself out of it—'

'If she told you, it isn't evidence that she did it, but we'll put it in because it's evidence she told you she did it.'

'Bugger evidence. It's what *happened.* Annette, why are you splitting hairs like this? Look, the lay-figure—'

'The *what*?'

And as Liz explained, Annette's professional impassivity giving way to disbelief, an unquenchable grin.

'All right, Annette, I know it's farcical. But, you see, everything was settling down; Reggie was in Cheltenham, out of the way, he couldn't be indiscreet, let the cat out of the bag. Helen was, well, holding everything together. At that point Paula didn't know, she hadn't quite worked it out—but, oh, yes, she was nearly there. She needed to—galvanise things. And, my God, she did. What was more publicised than Beattie's appearance? Yes? Paula, with all her busybodying amongst the underprivileged, knew where to go to buy that . . . thing. As for the clothes, Christ, have you seen her porch?'

Annette, mesmerised, catching up, nodded. Of course, it was all there: disguising waterproofs, Beattie's distinctive clothes . . .

Paula could fit herself out as whatever she wanted, whenever she wanted . . .

'Yes, Yes, Liz, I'm with you . . .'

'You see . . . She *made* something happen. I insisted Reggie come back to keep Helen company, and he did, and . . . Annette, she *used* me, and I was stupid enough to let her . . .'

'You were never stupid—'

'We got so close to it, didn't we? But it just never occurred to either of us that the man who was responsible for all this was dead— Helen's father, for God's sake. And Paula had known, all the time, like Helen, but without *knowing* she knew, without believing it was true, just an old man's maunderings . . .'

*   *   *

It was over two hours later when they left the interview room. Annette handed Liz a bunch of keys. 'Your aunt asked me to give you these. There's the front door and—'

'Yes, yes,' Liz murmured, her hand knowing the feel, the shape of them.

Hunter came down the corridor towards then. 'I had a devil of a job getting Miss Willoughby to have a solicitor.'

'Look, you must—'

'Liz, we are looking after her interests. She says she has no defence, no wish to escape justice, but I did manage to persuade her. Paula, on the other hand, is creating

280

seventeen kinds of shit. She wants her doctor, her MP, Civil Liberties, the Race Relations Board, Marriage Guidance, her husband, her daughters—'

'Oh, God,' Annette whispered, 'can we put sandbags round the nick?'

Liz said, 'She's a devious bitch, she'll try and wriggle out of everything.'

'No, she's off balance, she keeps changing her story, she doesn't seem to realise she's not making sense.'

'*Please let me see Helen.*'

'Yes, come on. We'll need to interview her again in a little while. You can have about twenty minutes.'

An interview room, smartly painted, brightly lit. A uniformed WPC sitting unobtrusively by the door.

This is the most heart-stopping moment of my life. No, I must think of her. She looked fragile, and very gentle, the least criminal of people imaginable. 'Helen . . .'

They sat side by side, holding hands tightly, unable to speak until Helen said steadily, 'I thought you would hate me . . .'

'Oh, how could I . . .'

And then there were words that had no meaning except in terms of comfort to one another. Helen was the first to sit a little straighter, begin to make sense. 'I'm to go before the magistrates on Monday. I won't get bail, no darling, don't have any false hopes on

281

that. We must be practical and deal with things as they are, not as we wish them to be, it's too late for that now.'

So they dealt with practical things: solicitors, accountants, the bank manager, relatives. Liz in a panic aware that their time was running out, wasted on the mundane 'I've asked if the vicar might visit me tomorrow, and it's perfectly all right. Would you go round when you leave, darling, and prepare him? I think,' Helen said, all her practicality lost in the mildest bemusement, 'this is the last place he would expect to see me. But everyone is so good. Do you know, I have to have eight hours uninterrupted sleep. I doubt I will, though, but there is a curious comfort in the thought that regulations require it. Now, Annette has given you the keys to Woodside . . . Good. I'm so glad you're friends, she's a splendid young person . . .'

'Yes,' Liz said, not daring to look up. *A splendid young person* . . . What did one do with standards no longer applicable, with unwanted tears.

'I am aware of the harm I've done you—no, listen. Barbara Devere is first class, we know, she would stand by you—'

'It's all right, I'll phone her this evening, and put my resignation in the post.'

'Darling, you love your job so much, it's not Barbara—'

'No, it's the parents. They're spending a

fortune having their girls taught history by a woman who—who—'

'Who has two relatives in custody, one for murder. This is what we have to do, face it, not evade it. I can only give you my heart's apology that you will have to cope with this alone.' With a glance towards the WPC, Helen lowered her voice—not concealment, but delicacy, this was a family matter. 'You know, I have thought for some time that Paula's mental state was rather precarious.'

'Yes, well . . . Helen, don't expect a charitable word from me about her. I admit I never knew about her financial difficulties— obviously they were fuel to her rage—that I was secure, that you were generous to me.'

'Darling, this is very important. That night, at Miller's Bridge, all I could think of was that I had to stop that woman destroying my life— and Reggie's—and yours.' She hesitated, looked intently at Liz. 'Don't you see—*I never even thought of Paula* . . . She has seldom entered into the least corner of my thoughts, and that night, she didn't exist for me. This is also something for which I must atone.'

'I won't have you taking it all on yourself. She started it—'

'No, Liz, my father started it. As your Mr Hunter said, *all those years ago.* Oh, my dear, don't cry. You can only see what I've lost. I've had so much happiness, Reggie, you . . . Now, darling, there's a price to pay . . .'

Liz found herself alone in a corridor. She leaned back against the wall, closed her eyes. She felt sad and confused, sick and angry.

A firm step. She opened her eyes.

'All right?' Hunter said.

She nodded.

'It meant so much to her, seeing you, knowing you hadn't—'

'I've really done it this time, haven't I? The wrong thing for the right reasons.'

'Liz, you had no control over any of this. You were caught up in it, and moved along, you'll begin to see that, when you've sorted it out in your mind.'

'Oh . . . don't you see . . . *she did it for me.*'

'She did it because of everything she is. Her past, her will to survive, her instinct for life. She wasn't herself, dear, dear girl.' How could he explain Helen to her, when she was so lost, so hurt—that he thought of Helen as the finest china—stand next to it, and the reality of his presence shattered it. 'Now, if you'll give me a few minutes, I'll take you home.'

'Woodside, please. I need to go to Woodside, there are things to do.'

She didn't hear his patient, 'Yes.' She was thinking of Woodside, its rooms full of light, the subtle harmony of its colours, its echoing emptiness.

His strong, cool hand was holding hers. There was no comfort there. She looked at him and saw on his face that he understood this. 'Give it time, Liz, give it time.'

She could think of nothing to say, only attempt an uncertain smile, and hold his hand a little more tightly.